Here Come the Bridesmaids!

Here Come the Bridesmaids!
Ann M. Martin

AN
APPLE
PAPERBACK

SCHOLASTIC INC.
New York Toronto London Auckland Sydney

Special thanks to Stuart Schultz of A Perfect Pear

No part of this publication may be reproduced in whole or in part, or stored in a retrieval system, or transmitted in any form or by any means, electronic, mechanical, photocopying, recording, or otherwise, without written permission of the publisher. For information regarding permission, write to Scholastic Inc., 555 Broadway, New York, NY 10012.

ISBN 0-590-48308-0

12 11 10 9 8 7 6 5 4 3   4 5 6 7 8 9/9

Printed in the U.S.A.   40

First Scholastic printing, December 1994

The author gratefully acknowledges
Peter Lerangis
for his help in
preparing this manuscript.

Here Come the Bridesmaids!

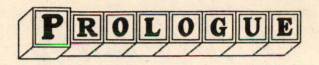

Dawn

My dad is getting married. I, Dawn Schafer, am going to be a bridesmaid.

Dad seems very happy about this.

Me? I'm a total wreck.

A few months ago, I was living in Stoneybrook, Connecticut, with my mom and stepfamily. Then I got permission to spend several months in California with my brother and divorced dad. Now, in December, right before I have to go back,

Dawn

Dad and his fiancée have planned The Day.

Not that I mind the _idea_ of remarriage. I don't. I'm used to it. My mom remarried, and that worked out great.

The problem isn't even Dad's bride to be. Not really. Although Carol takes a little getting used to. Okay, a lot of getting used to. She can be flakey. Plus she and Dad had a knock-down, drag-out fight not long ago. All of which doesn't seem to bode well for their future. But, hey, they're grown-ups. They say they've worked everything out. Besides, Carol's basically an okay person, and she'll be fine as a stepmom. Long-distance.

December is the problem.

Why? For one thing, it's the end of the semester. I have to pass all my courses if I want to move back to Connecticut. So I'll have to study like crazy for midterms, during all the wedding preparations.

But that's not the worst part. The worst part is that Mrs. Barrett is getting married to Franklin DeWitt in Connecticut <u>that same weekend.</u>

Huh? you may ask. What does this have to do with the price of clams in Cucamonga?

Nothing. It all has to do with the Baby-sitters Club. I belong to it, and so do my best friends in Stoneybrook. Mrs. Barrett and Franklin each have children, and the Barretts are major clients of ours. They've even asked some BSC members to help at the wedding ceremony.

Which means some of my friends will not be able to come to California for Dad's wedding.

Now, I adore Mrs. Barrett, her fiancé, and their kids. In fact, I would love to be at their wedding.

3

Dawn

_But why couldn't they
have planned it on a different
weekend?_

This is so frustrating!

Of course, I must control
myself. I can't expect all
my friends to be able to fly
cross-country for the wedding.
Besides, no one wants a
grump on such a happy
occasion.

So, to everyone on both
coasts, I am sweet, good-
natured, and thrilled.

Thank goodness I have a
journal, where I can write
how I really feel.

Which brings me to the
good news. I had the
greatest idea today.

Journals! One for each
wedding. I mean, if you
can't be someplace you
want to be, the next best
thing is reading about it.
I called my friends in
Connecticut during a BSC
meeting and mentioned
my idea. You know what

the answer was?

A loud YES!

We decided we'd each write down our own private thoughts. Then we'd collate them.

Everyone tried to think of a name for our two journals. Stacey McGill suggested BICOASTAL BELLS. Claudia Kishi thought up "I DO" X 4. Kristy Thomas loved EAST-WEST MARRI-AGE FEST.

I think, for now, I'll leave them without a title.

And I'll begin in California.

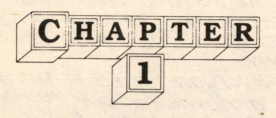

Dawn

Palo City, December 3
   Two weeks. Yikes! I am
soooooo excited. On
Saturday, December 17,
Dad and Carol will become
husband and wife. I
will have a new stepmother.
And I will make my
debut as a Radiant,
Luminous, and Up-to-the-
Minute Bridesmaid!...

Don't worry. I didn't make up that description. I got it from the tag on my bridesmaid's dress. I thought it sounded funny.

I wasn't the only one who thought so. Sunny Winslow howled when she read the tag in the store.

"Radiant and Luminous?" she blurted out. "That sounds like Wilbur the pig, from *Charlotte's Web!*"

"Huh?" said Maggie Blume.

Jill Henderson tapped her chin. "Radiant. That was one of the words Charlotte made in her web — to describe Wilbur."

"Huh?" Maggie repeated.

"You didn't *read* it?" Sunny asked with a look of utter disbelief.

Maggie shrugged. "I saw the video."

"Uh, guys?" I interrupted. "What do you think of the dress?"

Rule Number One of Dawn's Theory of Shopping: Never shop with best friends if you have something truly important to buy.

Rule Number Two: If you have to buy it during the holiday season, multiply Rule Number One by ten.

I discovered this at the Vista Hills mall on that Saturday morning. We arrived at 9:00. Mission: to find me a bridesmaid's dress.

Dawn

At 9:02 Sunny decided we needed extra energy for our quest. So we had granola and yogurt at a health-food snack bar called Health's Angels.

We left at 9:45 and ran into Chip Ransom, this ninth-grader who began flirting with Maggie while the rest of us stood around trying not to look *too* dorky.

At 9:50 Jill spotted the *perfect* tie for her father in a men's store window. Of course, we all went in to consult.

At 10:09, in front of SportsWest, Maggie remembered her uncle Lew's great love for golfing tees.

You get the picture.

When did we start looking for my dress? Noon. By that time, my friends were loaded down with Hanukkah and Christmas presents. Getting them to move was like pulling elephants across a swamp.

Actually, none of us is very elephantlike. We're all pretty normal thirteen-year-olds. Well, aside from the fact that each of us is a vegetarian, which some people find strange. (I find it strange to eat slaughtered animals.)

You know what else I find strange? Polluting our planet and destroying natural resources, such as trees. As you can guess, I am super-passionate about environmental issues. Here are some other things you need to know about me: I'm in eighth grade. I have long, light-blonde hair and freckles. And my life has been like a soap opera. "The Days of Dawn," in six scenes:

1. *Early Years.* I grow up happily in sunny, laid-back Palo City.

2. *The Divorce.* Mom decides to move back to her hometown (Stoneybrook) with me and my younger brother, Jeff. We buy an old farmhouse with a secret passageway that was once part of the Underground Railroad. I grow to love Stoneybrook, I meet great friends, and I join the Baby-sitters Club.

3. *The Big Split.* Jeff hates his new town and sinks into a huge funk. After much suffering, he decides he wants to live in California with Dad. Mom reluctantly agrees. (Two hankies for this part.)

4. *The Re-marriage.* My friend Mary Anne Spier and I discover that her dad used to date my mom in high school. We play matchmaker. They fall in love and get married — and the Spiers move into our house! (Swelling music here.)

5. *Dawn's Big Move.* I find myself missing Jeff and Dad terribly. I convince Mom and Richard (my stepfather) to let me move back to California for awhile. (More hankies.)

6. *California Wedding*. A work in progress. Sure to be another major tearjerker.

Hmm. Maybe I could get Maggie's dad interested in this plot. He's in The Industry. In Southern California talk, that means the movie business. You know what Maggie's favorite part of a movie is? The credits. She sits at the edge of her seat and reads the names of people she knows. (Me? I'm in the aisle, checking my watch.) Her style is more than cool. Hyper-cool. Robocool. Sometimes Maggie's outfits look totally bizarre, but then two weeks later, everyone else is wearing the same style. (I don't know how she does it.) Her hair is blonde, except for a small tail in back that's always dyed some color not found in nature. And her house — whoa. Bedrooms galore, two kitchens, a gym, a screening room, and a pool with a tropical landscape right out of *Gilligan's Island*. Glamorous, huh? But despite that, Maggie is down-to-earth and friendly.

Sunny is my closest friend in California. Her full name is Sunshine Daydream Winslow. (It's not her fault; her parents were hippies.) We both love surfing and ghost stories. Fortunately we also live in the same neighborhood. Her mom is the sweetest person, and she makes the most awesome pottery.

Jill Henderson lives way on the outskirts of

Palo City, with her mom (who's divorced) and her older sister, Liz. Oh, and also three ugly dogs, named Spike, Smee, and Shakespeare. (Maybe their parents were hippies, too.) Jill's the quietest of us all. She has deep brown eyes and dark blonde hair.

We four are known throughout the greater Palo City area as the We ♥ Kids Club. We've actually been in the local paper and on TV. But despite our great fame (ha ha), we are very easygoing. Our meetings are semi-regular, we have no officers, and hardly anyone arrives on time.

"Lazy slobs" is how Kristy Thomas would describe the W♥KC. Kristy lives in Stoneybrook, and she's the founder of the Babysitters Club. She set it up like a business, with herself as president. She's a born leader — loud, stubborn, and full of great ideas.

Sigh. I miss the BSC. It's much more structured than the W♥KC, but I love it just the same.

The Baby-sitters Club has regular meetings three times a week. Our clients (Stoneybrook parents) call during meeting times when they need baby-sitters. Everyone in the club has to arrive on time (or face the Wrath of Kristy), and everyone has a title. My stepsister, Mary Anne, is the club's secretary. She keeps the records and sets up all our sitting appointments. She and Kristy are best friends and sort of look-alikes. Both are short and have dark brown hair and eyes. But Mary Anne is quiet and sensitive, and that makes her . . . well, Kristy's opposite.

Stacey McGill is the treasurer. She's also a native New Yorker (and a divorced kid; her dad still lives in NYC). She's blonde and she has the most sophisticated sense of style. Like me, she eats only healthy food. She has to, because she has diabetes. If she has too much sugar, she could get really sick. (Don't worry. She's careful.)

Claudia Kishi's the vice-president, mainly because BSC meetings are held in her bedroom (she's the only member with a private phone). Claudia's a real artist. She can paint, draw, make jewelry, and put together the most creative outfits from odds and ends and old clothes. I love Claud, but I'll never understand two things about her: (1) She is a serious junk food addict, and (2) despite that, she's thin and healthy-looking. Gorgeous, too, with big almond-shaped eyes and jet-black hair (she's Japanese-American).

The BSC has two junior officers — Jessica Ramsey and Mallory Pike. They're in sixth grade (the rest of us are in eighth), and their parents won't allow them to baby-sit at night yet. Jessi's African-American, long-legged, elegant-looking, and a talented ballerina. Mallory's white, short, curly-haired, and determined to become a children's book writer someday. She's also the oldest of eight kids.

Until I left for California, I was the BSC's alternate officer. If someone was absent, I took over her job. What did the club do when I left? No problem. The BSC has two associate members, who aren't normally required to attend meetings. One of them, Shannon Kilbourne, took over for me. Shannon, who goes to Stoneybrook Day School, has curly blonde hair and a luminous and radiant smile. The other associate member is Mary Anne's boyfriend, Logan Bruno, who works baby-sitting around all his extracurricular sports activities.

Now you know all about me and my life. Well, the important stuff anyway.

Okay. Back to Saturday. We were in the "Bridal Trail" section of Carswell-Hayes, the anchor store of the mall.

The bridemaid's dress was a satiny material with shirred, off-shoulder sleeves, a fitted bodice, and a flared mid-calf skirt. The soft fuchsia color was just right for a wedding on the beach. (Yes, the beach. Isn't that cool?)

I tried it on and emerged from the dressing room to a chorus of oohs and aahs.

"It's gorgeous," Sunny said.

"Stunning," Maggie agreed.

"I was a bridesmaid once," Jill added, "with my sister. She picked the dress and it was *sooo* ugly. The worst thing was that she spent all this money on a dress she never wore again."

"Oh," I replied. Suddenly I wasn't so sure I wanted to buy it.

"But *this* one's different," Jill quickly said. "You could wear it a lot."

Sunny and Maggie nodded in agreement.

A saleswoman walked over to us and asked, "May I help you?"

I fingered the material. I was falling in love.

"I think she'll take it," Sunny said to the woman.

I wondered what Mary Anne would think. I spotted the same dress in her size on the rack. I wanted so badly to buy one for her. But would that be right? Shouldn't my co-bridesmaid be in on the decision? What if she hated it?

She couldn't.

"It's on sale, twenty percent off," the saleswoman said. "And it's returnable if you're not satisfied."

That did it. I took both dresses off the rack.

"I'll take two," I said to the woman.

"Yea!" Maggie exclaimed.

"Let's celebrate," Jill said.

"Lunch at Tito's Burritos!" Sunny suggested.

"No, Health's Angels," Maggie replied.

I let them fight it out while I paid for the dresses. All I could think about was the look on Mary Anne's face.

She was going to love it.

CHAPTER 2

Stacey

Stoneybrook, December 4
Snow alert! Yea!
Yes, snow. Sighted this morning.
Here in Stoneybrook. After a week
of tropical weather.
Okay, you could fly a 747 between
the flakes. And they melted as soon
as they touched the sidewalk. But the
important thing is — THE HOLIDAY
SEASON IS HERE!
♪♪ ♪♪ Oh, bring us some
♪ ♪♪ figgy pudding! ♪ #♪ ♪♪
(What is figgy pudding anyway?
It sounds revolting.)

Stacey

Anyway, I figured a little good cheer would help the beginning of this journal. Heaven knows I'm going to need it these next two weeks.

So are Mrs. Barrett and Franklin. After a day with the couple-to-be and their kids, I don't know how they're going to pull off this wedding in time. And still be talking to each other.

Oh, well, if things get tense, my mom knows a good divorce lawyer.
JUST KIDDING!
Actually, the story is MUCH happier than that . . . .

"Jingle bells, jingle bells, jingle all the way. Time to eat, have a seat, who wants scrambled eh-eggs?"

As I bounded into the kitchen, poor Mom was shuffling toward the coffee pot. She stopped and looked at me as if I'd gone completely crazy.

"Nine o'clock, time to rock, open up the fridge . . ." I sang.

I am not usually like this. Really. Snow does this to me. Besides, it was a Saturday. I had nothing to do except sit for the Barrett and

DeWitt kids. And THE SEASON had begun!

When we first moved to Stoneybrook, I thought the holidays would be bo-*ring*. No offense, but my old hometown is pretty amazing at this time of year. New York City, that is. The tree at Rockefeller Center, the department store windows, the smell of roasting chestnuts at every corner. . . .

I thought I'd never adjust to the "country." But you know what? I had a chance to live in New York again. After my family moved to Stoneybrook, we had to move *back* because of my dad's job. That's about when Mom and Dad started heading toward a divorce. Then I was faced with a choice — stay in NYC with Dad or return to Stoneybrook with Mom. And I chose Stoneybrook.

So the holidays aren't as flashy here. But hey, the snow on the ground stays white *much* longer. I never get stuck in the subway. Movie theater lines are shorter. And I get to hang out with my best friends in the world.

Plus I *love* baby-sitting, and as a Baby-sitters Club member, I do a lot of it.

That day, for example, I had been hired to keep the Barrett and DeWitt kids out of their parents' hair. The two families were going to visit their future house, to watch while the painters and decorators started work.

I was looking forward to it. I feel very close to the Barretts. I had been with them and the DeWitts when they picked out the house to begin with. I also spent two weeks last summer with the Barretts in Sea City, New Jersey (I was hired as mother's helper), where we all went through a hurricane together.

"Dutchess," mumbled Mom, with a mouthful of the omelette I'd made.

I assumed she was saying "Delicious," so I answered, "Thanks."

I was halfway through my own omelette when I heard a horn honking outside.

Mom scowled. "So early in the morning?" she grunted.

Ding-dong went the front door bell.

"Time to go!" I cleared my plate, grabbed my coat from the outside hallway, and ran to the front door.

"Did you take your medicine, sweetheart?" Mom called out.

"Yes, Mom."

"Bundle up!"

"Yes, Mom. 'Bye!"

My medicine, by the way, is insulin. It regulates the sugar in my bloodstream. Most people's bodies make their own insulin, but diabetics have to inject it daily. (Please don't barf. It's not as gross as it sounds.)

"Hi!" Buddy Barrett greeted me as I opened the door. "Lindsey was blowing the car horn. She's in big trouble."

Buddy is eight. Lindsey DeWitt is eight. Put them together and you get . . . big trouble. (Did you think I was going to say *sixteen*? Faked you out.)

Behind Buddy I heard squealing voices:

"I want to sit with Suzi!"

"Close the windows!"

"Ryan's drooling!"

By the curb in front of our house, kids were running back and forth between the Barrett sedan and the DeWitt station wagon. Mrs. Barrett and Franklin were standing outside, directing them like traffic police.

As Buddy and I walked toward the cars, I heard Suzi Barrett cry out, "Stacey sits with us!"

"Uh-uh! No way!" Taylor DeWitt retorted.

Suzi's five and Taylor's six. Usually Suzi is sweet-natured, but Taylor brings out her competitive side.

The other kids are Madeleine DeWitt (four), Marnie Barrett (two), and Ryan DeWitt (two).

From the expressions on the faces of the two grown-ups, I could see it had already been a long day.

"Hi, Stacey," Mrs. Barrett said with a tired

smile. "I hope you have a lot of energy today."

"Hop in," Franklin said, holding open the passenger door of the station wagon.

"No fair!" screamed Buddy.

I have never seen kids so noisy and excited. The new house was only about a half mile away, but I felt as if we were driving to Chicago.

As we pulled up in front of the house, the car doors flew open. Before I could unbuckle my seat belt, Buddy, Lindsey, Taylor, and Madeleine were running across the front lawn.

Next Suzi emerged, dragging a sleeping bag.

"What's that for?' I asked.

"To test the bedrooms," she replied. "So I know which one's best."

As she marched toward the house, I looked at Mrs. Barrett. She shrugged.

"It's locked!" Buddy shouted.

"Ee! Ee! Ee! Ee!" Marnie was shrieking with excitement in her car seat. I took her out, Franklin unbuckled Ryan, and Mrs. Barrett unlocked the front door.

Clomp-clomp-clomp-clomp! Footsteps echoed against the bare wood floors inside.

The house looked smaller than I'd remembered. It had two stories, a little patio out back, and a tiny front yard.

Marnie and Ryan seemed to find the pebbles on the driveway fascinating. I could hear Buddy making ghost noises in the attic. Lindsey and Taylor were opening and closing all the windows.

"The painters are due in fifteen minutes," Mr. DeWitt said. "The kids have to be out of their way."

"Okay," I replied.

Well, fifteen minutes passed by. Then twenty. Then a half hour.

I ran in and out of the house. I broke up a fight between Buddy and Taylor. I tried to explain to Suzi why she wouldn't be able to sleep in the kitchen. I supervised the two toddlers when they decided to walk up and down the front steps a million times.

The workers arrived forty minutes late. Mrs. Barrett had this tight little smile on her face. I recognized it. I had seen it in Sea City when she was about to fly into a rage.

I was glad I wasn't one of those workers.

"Come on, guys!" I called into the house. "Time to go outside."

Buddy came running up from the basement, just as Suzi was walking through the living room. "I saw a rat downstairs!" Buddy announced.

"A *what*?" Mrs. Barrett, Mr. DeWitt, one of the workers, and I asked all at once.

Suzi was goggle-eyed. Buddy approached her, holding his fingers to his mouth like fangs. "It had these sharp, sharp teeth, and it said, 'Where's Suzi? Where's Suzi?'"

Suzi burst into tears and ran out of the house. *"Mo-o-o-om!"*

"Hamilton Barrett, you come over here this instant!" Mrs. Barrett commanded.

The next few hours passed in a blur. The workers marched in and out of the house with paint supplies, wallpaper, and ladders. I set up games of red light-green light, tag, duck-duck-goose, and anything I could think of. We went on a backyard treasure hunt and found a golf ball, an interesting rock, and an empty film cannister.

Franklin nearly exploded when one of the workers accidentally put a hole in the kitchen wall. Mrs. Barrett hated the new living room wallpaper and insisted on switching it. Madeleine managed to sneak inside and came out screaming, with a hand covered in plaster.

Lindsey yelled at Madeleine. Mrs. Barrett yelled at me. Franklin yelled at Mrs. Barrett.

The workers yelled at each other. When I tried to take Madeleine into the basement to wash her hands in the industrial sink, she freaked out. "I hate rats!" she screamed. Buddy thought this was hysterical.

By lunchtime, I felt like an overcooked lasagna noodle, limp and flat.

Mr. DeWitt walked out the back door, white flecks of paint in his hair. "Who wants to go to Burger Town?"

The kids ran to the cars, yelling with excitement. Me? I kept my cool. I followed them quietly. I helped them settle in the car.

But I could not wait to sit indoors with a nice, big, greasy cheeseburger.

"The kitchen is too dark, sweetheart," Mrs. Barrett said, taking a french fry from her bag.

"More mee-oke!" Ryan demanded. (Translation: more milk.)

"But we decided on the color long ago," Franklin protested.

"It'll cover up food stains better," Lindsey suggested.

"Oh? Do you plan to fling food at the wall?" Franklin asked.

"I do!" Buddy piped up.

"Eat your burger," I urged him.

"Did you call the tux rental place?" Mrs. Barrett asked Franklin.

His face fell. "Oops."

"We have to be on top of these things, Franklin," Mrs. Barrett said.

"I know, I know," he said sheepishly.

"I've ordered all my bridesmaids' dresses except Stacey's."

I nearly choked on a pickle slice. "Huh?"

"What are you, a size six?" Mrs. Barrett asked.

I swallowed. "You want me to be a — a — *bridesmaid*?"

"Oh, dear . . . You mean, I didn't tell you?"

A grin slowly spread across Franklin's face. "Harrumph," he said. "On top of things?"

Mrs. Barrett blushed. "I'm awfully sorry. We've been so frantic! You see, Stacey, one of my college friends had agreed to be a bridesmaid, but the other day she canceled. Would you like to take her place? You've been like part of our family."

My mind was in the ozone layer. The kids could have been pelting each other with chicken nuggets and I wouldn't have noticed.

I love weddings. I cry just thinking about them. My eyes were starting to water already.

Me? A bridesmaid? I would be part of their

most precious memory. Every time they opened up their wedding album, there I'd be, forever thirteen.

Would I?

"Of course I will!" I replied. "I mean, if my mom lets me."

Mrs. Barrett was grinning. "Have her call me if there's any problem."

Buddy and Lindsey were arguing. Straw wrappers flew around me. Seven rambunctious kids were turning Burger Town into a war zone.

I didn't mind at all.

The whole crazy day was worth it.

CHAPTER 3

Jessi

Stoneybrook, December 7
Ho! Ho! Ho!
Guess what I'm
going to be doing
this holiday season?
I know, I know.
I'm supposed to
write about the
wedding. But I
can't. At least not
in this entry. Not
after what happened
today....

"Chestnuts roasting on an open fire . . ." warbled Mallory Pike.

"Aw-rooooo!" howled Kristy Thomas.

"Auughhh!" Claudia Kishi picked up two pillows and pressed them against her ears.

Mallory was unfazed. "Jack Frost nipping off your nose . . ."

"*At,*" Shannon Kilbourne reprimanded gently. " 'Nipping *at* your nose,' Mal, not *off.*"

"That's disgusting," Kristy said.

The rest of us were giggling uncontrollably.

"Yuletide carols being flung in the fire. . . ."

"Okay, okay." Shannon could barely keep a straight face. "I take it back. You were right. You *can't* sing."

Mal was blushing, but she had this sly smile on her face.

Shannon had asked for it. She'd been trying to get us all to sing carols, which is a little like trying to get rhinos to tap dance. Reluctantly we joined in — except for Mallory, who claimed her voice was too awful. So Shannon made it her mission to convince Mal she could really sing.

Did Mallory shrink away? No. She put on a comedy act.

"They know that Santa's on his way; he's

loaded lots of poison goodies on his sleigh. . . ."

Where was she getting this stuff? We were laughing so hard, we were snorting.

Welcome to a meeting of the Baby-sitters Club.

Believe it or not, we can be serious. We were just in a silly mood that day. Holiday spirit, I guess. Besides, eleven minutes had gone by and not one parent had called.

Eleven minutes may not sound like a long time, but our meetings only last half an hour: 5:30 to 6:00 (on Mondays, Wednesdays, and Fridays).

At 5:43, the phone finally rang.

"Sshhhh!" Claudia urged. We held in our giggles as she lifted the receiver. "Hello, Baby-sitters Club. Oh, hi, Mrs. McGill. . . . She's right here."

Stacey's mom works at a department store called Bellair's. Sometimes she calls during the BSC meeting to tell Stacey she'll be late. "Hi, Mom," Stacey said cheerfully into the receiver. "Is everything okay? . . . You're looking for a *what*? When? Okay, I will. . . . Thanks."

We all stared at Stace as she hung up. She looked totally confused. "That's weird. She called to say they lost their Santa Claus."

Huh?

"Disappeared between men's shoes and home appliances, huh?" Claudia said solemnly. "I know that area. It's like the Bermuda Triangle."

"No." Stacey smiled. "The guy who's playing their Santa is this actor, and he got cast in a movie, so he has to leave town right away. Mom tried calling some backups, but they're all busy playing Santa in other places."

Kristy's mind went to work. "Well, I'm sure if they put an ad in the paper, maybe checked with some employment agencies — "

"It's too late for the ad," Stacey interrupted. "And I don't think an agency would help because it's a volunteer job. She asked if one of *us* wanted to do it, starting a week from Saturday."

Claudia nearly choked on a Cheez Doodle. "You're joking."

"Better keep eating," Kristy remarked. "You may need a big belly."

"Very funny," Claudia replied. "Like a thirteen-year-old girl is really going to be a Santa."

"Mom says it doesn't matter," Stacey insisted. "The most important thing is caring about kids."

"I don't know," Mary Anne said. "I mean, what about our height, our voices — "

"Santa doesn't have to be super-tall. And you can lower your voice," Mallory suggested.

We stared at each other for a moment.

"Uh, don't all volunteer at once," Claudia murmured.

"It'll be four hours next Saturday and Sunday," Stacey said. "It's not a big deal, like Macy's. All you do is ring a bell and walk around the third floor, talking to kids."

Kristy chimed in, "Check the schedule. See who's available."

Mary Anne flipped through our calendar. "Well, I'm going to California, and so are Kristy and Claudia. Mal's got the Prezziosos Sunday afternoon. Shannon has the Papadakises. . . ."

I knew this was going to happen. I could feel it. Everyone was looking at me. My stomach began to rumble.

I was trapped.

"Uh, guys, I can't," I squeaked.

"Why not?" Kristy demanded.

"Three small things," I replied. "I'm eleven years old. I'm a girl. And I'm black. Remember?"

"So?" Claudia said. "I'd do it if I could."

I raised my eyebrow. "Uh-huh. Right."

I should mention that when my family first moved to Stoneybrook, we felt like aliens.

Some people did not accept us at all.

"You shouldn't think about race," Claudia went on. "Kids aren't prejudiced the way grown-ups are."

"Besides, who says Santa can't be black?" asked Shannon.

"That's true," I said. Besides, *I* always liked seeing African-American Santas in Oakley, New Jersey, where I grew up. Sure, that was a racially mixed town compared to Stoneybrook, but why shouldn't children of color *here* have someone to look up to? Not necessarily *me*, but —

"So you'll do it?" Stacey asked.

"I didn't say that!" I protested.

"Come on . . ." Shannon teased. "Think of those kids."

"It'd be fun," Mary Anne said.

It did sound like fun. Sort of.

I shrugged. "I don't know . . ."

"Yes!" Kristy shouted. "I knew she'd do it!"

"Wait!"

Too late. Stacey called back her mom, who said I should go for a fitting after the meeting.

Feeling numb, I called my dad and told him what had happened.

He roared with laughter. "That's something *I* should be doing!"

"Would you?" I asked hopefully.

"I don't have the time, sweetheart. But I'll take you to Bellair's, if that's what you want."

And that is how I, Jessica Ramsey, became a department store Santa Claus.

I arrived at Bellair's by 6:21. Mrs. McGill met me and took me to a locker room area. There I met a woman named Ms. Javorsky, who was in charge of fitting me.

She did not pass out when she saw me. She didn't even laugh. In fact, she seemed thrilled.

"You are a life saver, my dear," she said to me. "You have no idea how happy we are."

"You don't mind that I'm not . . ."

"A roly-poly old man with a beard and a jolly laugh?" Ms. Javorsky laughed. "Do you know how hard it is to get someone like that to volunteer on a weekend during the holidays? Last year's Santa was a high school boy with an earring and hair past his shoulders. He kept saying, 'Yo, what's up?' to the kids, instead of 'Ho, ho, ho.'"

"And you didn't mind?"

"Not at all. He was so charming, and the children *adored* him." Ms. Javorsky gave me a reassuring smile. "If the little ones see through the disguise, they just make up their own explanations — you're Santa's helper or something. And the big ones already know the truth anyway, so it doesn't matter who you are."

"I guess . . ."

"Don't you worry. Now, up up up!"

She gestured to a small stool. I climbed it and she quickly took my measurements with a tape.

When she finished, she shook her head and chuckled. "Well, I'll be doing a lot of hemming. And you'll need plenty of padding. Okay, let's work a little on the delivery."

She pulled a fake beard and a hat off the shelf. I put them on and tried to jut out my belly.

I felt like a fool.

"Um, what do I . . ."

"Hi, Santa!" Ms. Javorsky blurted out. "I'm so happy to meet you!"

"Uh, ho ho ho! What would you like this year?"

"Well, a Porsche would be nice," Ms. Javorsky replied with a grin.

"I'll have a little trouble getting that down the chimney," I said, stroking the beard. "How about some socks?"

Ms. Javorsky burst out laughing. "Perfect!"

"Really?" I said. "That's all I need to do?"

With a big grin, she held out her hand. "Welcome to Bellair's, Santa!"

That did it. I was psyched. Bellair's was going to get the best Santa Claus they'd ever seen!

CHAPTER 4

Mallory ☺

Stoneybrook, December 10

Boy, am I in trouble. I never should have opened my big mouth in the BSC meeting. Then I wouldn't have had my great idea at the Hobarts' today. But I did, and I did, and now my life is a total mess....

It started out so innocently.

I was at Ben Hobart's house that Saturday. Ben's sort of my boyfriend. I mean, we don't exactly call each other boyfriend and girlfriend (I'm not sure why). But we do hang out and go to school dances together. And you know what? I even turned down a date with a really cute fifteen-year-old guy this past summer because of Ben.

If that's not boyfriend and girlfriend, I don't know what is.

Ben has a medium-size family. Well, to *me* it's medium. You might think otherwise. He has three younger brothers: James is eight, Mathew six, and Johnny four. All the Hobart boys have reddish-blond hair, round faces, and freckles.

You know what the cutest thing about them is? Their accents. They were born in Australia, and they say things like "hoi" for *hi*, "g'die" for *good day*, and "jumper" for *sweater*. Ben calls me "Mel-ry."

Anyway, we weren't doing anything special, just talking in the kitchen. Mr. Hobart was in the basement repairing something, Mrs. Hobart had gone off to do some errands, and Ben's brothers were running in and out of the house.

It was cloudy and pretty warm for a winter day. Even from the kitchen, I could hear neighborhood kids playing outside.

"Ben and Mel-ry sitting in a tree . . ." James sang as he darted out the rec room and toward the back door.

"Watch it!" Ben shot back. "If you want anything for Christmas."

James turned and smirked at him. "You can't fool me with that anymore!"

He had this funny look on his face. I recognized it. It was saying, *I know there's no Santa Claus, but I'm not going to say it, because my little brothers might hear.* (As you might guess, I see this expression in my family a lot.)

"Yeah?" Ben said. "Well, don't forget, *I* buy presents, too, for people who deserve them."

James's smirk disappeared. "Sorry."

As he slunk out the door, Ben sighed. "Do you get presents for all your brothers and sisters?"

I nodded. "I buy things here and there, all through the year — little things. Last year I got Claire a hole puncher and it was her favorite gift."

"Yeah?"

Johnny barged inside, screaming. Behind him was Jamie Newton, another four-year-old who lives in the neighborhood. Jamie was making these timid little roaring noises and giggling.

A moment later, Mathew walked in with Myriah Perkins from next door. They were gabbing about some video game.

Ben and I tried to move away from the kitchen, but we couldn't. The kids kept asking for juice, snacks, and all sorts of things they couldn't reach.

Finally Ben suggested, "How about a big pot of hot chocolate?"

"Yeaaaaaaa!"

Ding-dong. As we were assembling the ingredients, the front doorbell rang. Mathew, Myriah, Johnny, and Jamie all ran to answer it.

It was Charlotte Johanssen and Becca Ramsey (Jessi's sister). "Hi, guys!" Becca called out. "Where's James?"

James ran in from the back, followed by Jake Kuhn. "Hi!" James greeted them. "Me and Jake found a birds' nest!"

"Let's see!"

The kids stampeded toward the back door. There they practically collided with Mr. Hobart, who had clomped up from the basement. "Well, well," he exclaimed. "Welcome to the circus. Do your parents all know you're here?"

A chorus of yeses rang out.

"What about the hot chocolate?" I asked.

A door slam was my answer. Mr. Hobart shrugged and said, "Leave the window open. Soon as they smell it, they'll come running back."

He was right. And when they returned, Nina Marshall had joined them (she's four).

Now I felt at home. *Nine* kids.

You should have seen them. You'd think they hadn't eaten or drunk in weeks.

"Me first!"

"Give me some!"

"Quit pushing!"

Ben finally boomed, "Wait a minute! I'll serve whoever's sitting down!"

Zoom. Musical chairs. James, Jake, Johnny, Becca, Nina, and Myriah grabbed the six kitchen chairs. Mathew scrambled into the dining room and dragged in two more chairs, while Charlotte got the piano bench for Jamie.

Ben thought this was hilarious. As he ladled the hot chocolate, he began singing, "Deck the halls with boughs of holly." (Ben loves to sing.)

"Fa-la-la-la-la, la-la-la-la," Myriah, Johnny, and Charlotte joined in.

"Come on, everybody!" Ben urged.

Jake blushed. Becca rolled her eyes. Nina began moving her mouth, but nothing came out.

"If you want to have hot chocolate, fa-la-la-la-la, la-la-la-la," Ben continued in this goofy voice, "you must sing these Christmas carols, fa-la-la-la-la, la-la-la-la."

Ben was being unfair. Some of those kids are super-shy. He was tormenting them!

But you know what? One by one, they all started singing. Even Nina. It was a little like the Whos, in *How the Grinch Stole Christmas*.

As for me, quiet Mallory Pike? Well, I guess my performance at the Baby-sitters Club meeting had loosened me up. I sang out, horrible voice and all.

When we finished the verse, Mathew asked, "What comes next?"

"Wait." Ben ran into the living room and returned with a big book of carols. He flipped through the pages and said, "Um, here it is. 'Fast away the old year passes.'"

We sang through the whole song, with Ben calling out the words in advance. By the end of it, everyone was smiling. The kids wore these little brown hot-chocolate mustaches.

"This is *fun!*" Jamie exclaimed.

"Remember last year, when those kids went from door to door, singing carols?" Charlotte said.

"They came to our house," Jake said, "and my mom invited them in for cookies."

"Can *we* do that?" James asked.

"Go caroling?" I replied. "You really *want* to?"

"Yeeeeaaaahhh!" It was unanimous.

Ben and I looked at each other. "When?" he muttered.

"Closer to Christmas, like next Saturday," I suggested.

"Yeeeeaaaahhh!"

The kids were jumping up and down. Nina's hot chocolate mug went flying (fortunately it was empty and plastic).

"Sounds good to me," Ben said, paging through the book again. "I guess we better keep practicing. Okay, how about 'Rudolph the Red-Nosed Reindeer'?"

Well, we got through that one, and "Silent Night," and "Oh, Hanukkah," and "We Wish You a Merry Christmas," and a couple of others.

Halfway through "We Three Kings," I

caught a glimpse of the stove clock turning to
12:27.

I was due home at 12:15.

"Oops, I have to go!" I blurted out.

Ben looked disappointed. He walked me to
the door, while the kids scattered.

"I don't know about this," Ben said. "What
if the kids get too shy again? What if we don't
sound good?"

"Don't worry, it'll be great," I said. " 'Bye!"

" 'Bye."

What's the worst thing about having seven
siblings? Sometimes your parents don't even
know you're alive.

What's the best thing? Sometimes your parents don't even know you're alive.

When I got home, Dad was busy chewing
out three of my brothers while Mom was doing
an art project in the basement with the rest of
my sibs.

I slipped right in the back door, twenty minutes late. No one said a word.

Quickly I tiptoed to my room. When the
phone rang, I called out, "I'll get it!" as if I'd
been in the house for hours.

I picked up the phone in my parents' room.
"Hello?"

"Mallory? Hi, it's Claudia! Guess who just called me?"

"Who?"

"Mrs. Barrett."

Sometimes BSC clients call during non-meeting times. It's usually an emergency, which means Claudia has to call around frantically.

"She's, like, hysterical," Claudia continued. "I had to listen to a lecture about bad caterers. Then she tells me every single thing going wrong with the wedding plans. Finally she says she totally forgot about all the kids who are coming to the wedding. What if they make too much noise? What if they get hungry?"

"So she needs a sitter?"

"Two. I already lined up Shannon, but no one else can do it."

"I can!" I exclaimed.

"Great," Claudia replied. "Thanks. We'll talk later. I'm going to call her right now. 'Bye."

" 'Bye."

How cool.

I was going to be part of the wedding. Official Keeper of the Kids. Maybe I could stand in the receiving line with the families.

I began dancing around the bedroom. I began thinking about a beautiful dress I'd seen at Steven E, a store in the mall. Maybe I'd be allowed to buy it for the wedding. I had a whole week to convince Mom and Dad.

I froze.

A week from today. That was the day of the wedding.

Saturday.

The same day as the Christmas caroling I'd just planned.

Uh-oh.

I picked up the phone and began tapping out Claudia's number.

"Hey! Quit it!" shouted my brother, Adam, over the phone. "I'm talking!"

I was about to yell at him, tell him to get off, but I didn't. I just said "Sorry" and hung up.

It was no use. Claudia was already calling Mrs. Barrett. Confirming the appointment.

One thing you never, ever do as a BSC member is cancel an appointment — unless you have somebody to cover for you. (Even then Kristy chews you out.)

With a sigh, I slumped onto the bed. I was

stuck. I was going to have to let down all those kids.

Well, maybe not. We hadn't said we were *definitely* doing it. Had we?

I waited a few minutes and picked up the phone again. Adam was finished, so I called Ben.

I explained everything to him. I hoped he wouldn't be too mad.

The first thing he said was, "Cancel it."

"Cancel my job?" I asked. "I can't do that."

"Well, you said you'd do this first."

"Yeah, but this is a *job*."

"So? What am I going to tell the kids?"

"Ben, we said we'd *think* about caroling. We didn't say we would *do* it!"

"Tell them that. My brothers have been practicing! They can't wait."

I fell silent. I could hear Ben breathing like an angry bull. "I . . . I don't know what to say," I murmured.

"So you're going to cancel on us?" Now he was practically shouting.

"I have to, Ben."

"Fine. Great. Whatever."

Click.

I stared at the receiver, gaping.

He *hung up* on me. Just slammed the phone

down without saying good-bye.

What a jerk.

I slammed the phone down, too. Let him take the kids by himself. Let him do whatever he wanted by himself.

No way was I ever going to talk to him again.

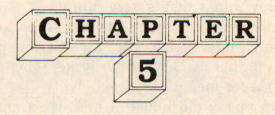

CHAPTER 5

SUZI

Stoneybrook, December 12
    My mommy is getting married.
We will be living in a new house.
It is ugly and broken down. It needs
to be painted and fixed. We should
not move there until December 26.
Then it will be better. . . .

Suzi

You know what Stacey calls me? A little dictator. Because I dictated my entry to her.

Stacey thinks that is very funny.

I know how to write. But it takes too long. Anyway, I *really* like the way Stacey puts hearts on her *i*'s. So I let her write, when she baby-sat for me.

I am in my old house. I miss it so much. Even though I still live here. That's because my family will be moving. So we're kind of connected to the new house now.

I miss my old bed, too. I'm going to sleep on a bunk bed in the new house, with Madeleine, my new sister. She's only four. I'm five and five-twelfths.

Know what else? Soon I will have *two* daddies. My new one is named Franklin. Maybe he is related to Benjamin Franklin. I asked him that once, and he just laughed. But he did not say no.

My old daddy got a divorce. He lives in Milwaukee now. That's far away. Like a million miles, or maybe even a thousand. But not a googolplex. That's the highest number in the universe. My big brother, Buddy, told me.

I miss my old daddy even more than my old house and bed.

The new house is yucky. I do not *not* NOT want to move there.

We went there the day before yesterday with my new daddy's kids. Stacey went with us, but she mostly played with Marnie and Ryan. The house smelled like paint. Ick! And the kitchen wallpaper had pictures of broccoli on it. So we have to look at it while we eat. That is so disgusting. One of the bathrooms has a gross hole in the ground instead of a toilet. Franklin said the plumbers were coming to put in a new one.

The ceilings have holes, too, with wires coming out of them. Buddy said they were alien monster claws, and I got scared. Mommy yelled at him. He's mean to me.

I thought I heard a rat downstairs, too, but Mommy told me to shush.

I shushed. I walked through the house. I saw the new carpet in my bedroom. Madeleine turned on the shower by mistake and got wet. Taylor and me slid on the shiny living room floor.

We bonked against one wall. Then we bonked against the other, and the other, and the wall with windows. And then I noticed THE MOST HORRIBLE THING.

"Mommy?" I called out. *"Mommy!"*

Mommy came walking in. "What?"

"They covered up the fireplace."

"What are you talking about?"

"The workers. They put plaster over the fireplace. Look!" I pointed to the long, blank wall at the end of the room. Where the fireplace is in our old house.

Mommy sighed. "Suzi, nobody covered anything. This house has no chimney."

"It doesn't?"

"Duh," Buddy said. I didn't even see him come into the room.

"Duh to you!" Taylor yelled back.

"Buddy," Mommy said warningly, "you leave your sister alo — "

"But what about Santa?" I asked.

"What *about* him?" Mommy asked.

"Where will he come in?"

Mommy didn't say anything. She looked at the wall. Then she looked around the living room. "Well . . ."

Taylor started biting his fingernails.

"Through the hole in the bathroom floor," Buddy said.

"Eeeewww!" Lindsey started laughing. She was in the hallway, behind Cruddy Buddy.

"The window," Mommy said. "We'll leave the window open."

I looked out the living room window. "You

mean, the reindeer will land on the lawn?"

Buddy started laughing really loud.

"Buddy, will you please go play somewhere else?" Mommy asked.

My brother doesn't believe in Santa Claus. But Santa still brings him presents. That is so unfair.

"Hey, wait up!" Taylor called out. He ran after Buddy.

I can't believe Taylor likes my brother so much, when Buddy is so mean.

"They can eat some grass," I said to Mommy.

"Huh?" she asked.

"The reindeer. While they're waiting."

Mommy smiled and gave me a kiss. Then she went into the kitchen.

I looked at the window. I could put milk and cookies on the sill. Santa would see them there.

But then I thought of something else.

"Mommy!"

Mommy came back in again. She had a tape measure in her hand. "What is it, sweetie?"

"Did you tell Santa we moved?"

"Tell him? Uh, I suppose he has a list or something . . ."

"What if he looks for us in our old house?"

"Suzi — "

"We won't be there! He'll think we died and he'll give my toys to somebody else."

I started crying. Mommy sat on the floor against the wall with no fireplace. She held out her arms and I ran to her.

"I don't want to live in this stupid house!" I said.

Mommy rocked me back and forth. "Let's see," she said. "How can we solve this problem?"

We thought a minute.

"What about, like, those planes on the beach?" I suggested. "You know, the ones pulling the signs? We could get one with our address on it."

"Uh, er," Mommy said.

"But then a robber might see it," I realized.

"Good point."

"Mommy, how many days till Christmas Eve?"

"Twelve."

"How long does it take a letter to get to the North Pole?"

Mommy smiled. "Oh, four or five. Maybe a week."

"*Yes!* Can we write Santa a letter?"

"Sure, Suzi. As soon as we get home. Maybe Stacey can help you. She's baby-sitting to-night."

"Okay!"
Whew. Did I feel better.

Dear Santa,
Hi. I do not live in the same house. My new address is 48 Chestnut Drive. It's the house with the white shingles. There's no chimney so use the window. Leave the reindeer on the lawn. They can eat some grass.
Don't give my toys to the people who move into our old house, okay?
Love,

SUZI BARRETT

P.S. Please write back!

Like my letter? Mommy and I made a copy of it the next day. Then we went to the post office and mailed it.

"Are you happy now, sweetheart?" asked my mommy.

"Yes," I said. But I wasn't. "Mommy?"

"Uh-huh?"

"How many kids are in the world? A googolplex?"

"No, but millions. Maybe billions."

"How much room does a million letters take?"

"I don't know, Suzi. A few rooms, I guess."

"Oh."

A few rooms?

Santa could *never* read that many letters! What if he didn't read mine?

"Mommy?"

"Suzi. I'm driving —"

I was so angry. "We can't move until after Christmas!"

"We just mailed your letter."

"The house is yucky. You can move there. I am staying home!" I folded my arms.

We didn't say another word the whole trip.

CHAPTER 6

Mary Anne

Stoneybrook, December 15

Hi! Here is my last
entry in this journal.
Everything is packed,
including my beautiful
plaid dress for the
wedding. 'Bye, room, 'Bye,
Stoneybrook. In about
three hours I will be
sitting with Kristy and
Claudia on an airplane.
California, here we come!

"Done," I said to myself.

I shut the journal. I ran my finger down my list of things to do. WRITE JOURNAL ENTRY was the second to last thing. I crossed it off.

The last thing on the list was KISS TIGGER GOOD-BYE.

Tigger is my kitten. He's gray and white and my absolute favorite creature on the whole earth.

I know he sensed what was going to happen. He had this sad look in his eyes, and he hadn't let me out of his sight since I'd gotten home from school.

"Ohhhh, Tiggy." I picked him up and wrapped him in my arms.

Meeeeew? he said with this fragile, confused tone.

Forget it. I could feel my heart just fall apart. Tears swam down my cheeks. "I'll be back."

We stayed like that for awhile. Then I looked at my clock. Four-fifteen. Our plane was due to leave at seven, and we needed to allow time to get to the airport and pick up our tickets.

I put Tigger down gently and ran downstairs. "Dad? Sharon? I'm ready."

Dad appeared at the foot of the stairs, looking at his watch. "Uh, we're not driving to California, honey. We have a few hours."

"But we have to pick up Kristy and Claudia," I said, "and what if we hit traffic on the way to the airport?"

Dad sighed and began trudging upward. "Okay, I'll bring down your suitcase. Since you want to leave us so badly — "

"No, I don't. It's just that — "

Sniff, sniff. Dad was pretending to cry. I could see his lips curling up into a smile.

From the kitchen, my stepmother called, "Richard, stop it."

Sharon was smiling. (So was I. Dad can be pretty goofy when he wants to, but we still love him.) She was busily packing a lunch bag. "Brownies for your trip," she said. "You don't get much to eat on these flights."

"Great." I tried to sound enthusiastic. The last time Sharon made brownies, she forgot to put in eggs. They tasted like chocolate rubber. (Sharon is soooo sweet, but she can be a little absent-minded.)

She must have read my mind. "Don't worry," she said. "I bought them."

As she turned to look at me, she tried to smile. But I could see tears in her eyes.

Me? I started blubbering again. We fell into each other's arms. "It's — it's only for nine days," I said between sobs. "Then Dawn and I will *both* be home."

60

"I know," Sharon whispered.

Poor Sharon. She sure had had her share of painful good-byes. First her divorce, then Jeff moving back to California with his dad, then Dawn's long visit there.

Somehow I hadn't thought my trip would mean that much to her. But it did.

And it made me realize just how close we'd grown.

I could hear Dad's footsteps booming down the stairs. "What did you pack in here, cement?" he grunted. When he reached the bottom step, he let the suitcase thump to the floor. Then he began flexing his arm. "Do I look like Ah-nold?" he asked, in a terrible Arnold Schwarzenegger imitation.

Leave it to my dad. Sharon and I cracked up. I wiped my eyes, then quickly called Kristy and Claudia.

Dad, Sharon, and I went out to the car, put my suitcase in the trunk, and took off.

First we arrived at Claudia's house. "Hi!" she squealed from the front door as we pulled up.

She and her dad were each holding luggage as they came out of the house. Her sister and mom followed behind them, lugging an overstuffed, belted-together suitcase. They looked as if they were trying to drag out a hippo.

"Is the whole *family* going?" Dad asked me quietly.

"Uh, I don't think so," I replied.

As Claudia ran to me, Dad got out to open the trunk. I could hear him grumble something about renting a moving van.

Claudia and I hugged excitedly. "Oh, I have to ask you," she said. "Did you bring a lined raincoat? I mean, I know it sometimes gets cold at night, so I brought a few sweaters. And I know it doesn't rain much, but I did bring a slicker just in case. And some boots for the mud. But if it rains at *night* . . ."

Thud!

Thud!

WHOOMP!

Claudia's suitcases landed in our trunk.

"I think you're prepared for anything," I said.

She hugged her parents and sister. Everyone said good-byes.

We gabbed nonstop in the car. Soon we were pulling up to Kristy's house, which is in Stoneybrook's wealthy neighborhood.

No, Kristy is not a rich snobby type. Far from it. Most of her life she lived in a normal house across the street from Claudia. Her dad abandoned the family when she was little (yes, abandoned, without even a good-bye), so her

62

mom had to raise Kristy and her three brothers — Charlie (who's now seventeen), Sam (fifteen), and David Michael (seven). In fact, Kristy dreamed up the idea for the Baby-sitters Club because she saw how tough it was for her mom to get a sitter.

How did everything change for Kristy? It's right out of a soap opera. Mrs. Thomas met this nice guy named Watson Brewer, who happened to be a millionaire. So Kristy got a new dad, a mansion to live in, two stepsiblings (Karen and Andrew), and later an adopted sister (Emily Michelle).

And they were all there to say good-bye when we arrived. Kristy came bounding down the front steps with a duffel bag slung over her shoulder.

"Is that *it*?" Claudia asked.

Kristy shrugged. "I'm not *moving*." And that was that.

To a loud chorus of " 'byes" and "have funs," we drove off.

On the highway we played a memory game called "I Packed My Grandmother's Trunk." Everyone has to add one item, but only after repeating every item that's already been added.

By the time we got to the airport, we had packed (among other things) a bathtub, a flugelhorn, five frozen dinners, a dead wombat, a year's supply of toilet paper, and a collapsible helicopter. (Don't ask me.)

It was 5:30 when we got on the ticket line. The terminal was *packed*. Kids were squirming in their down coats, couples were crying, huge families were wandering around like schools of fish.

At the ticket counter, Kristy had to pretend one of Claudia's suitcases was hers, so Claudia wouldn't be charged for overweight luggage. We took our tickets and ran toward the gate.

Except for Claudia. She ran to the snack shop.

After eating a few Goobers and Heath Bars, and after another flurry of tearful goodbyes, we were in the plane, sliding into our seats.

My heart was pounding. My stomach was in a knot. I could barely speak. Claudia and Kristy were giggling for no special reason.

This was it.

We were on our way to California, JUST US!

Kristy got the window seat, but we all crowded around her. We spotted Sharon and Dad looking for us through the waiting room window, arm in arm. We waved, but I don't think they saw us.

Ding, went a soft bell.

"Ladies and gentlemen, welcome to Flight 403 to Los Angeles," an official-sounding voice announced. "If you'll turn to the front of the cabin, the flight attendants will demonstrate the safety procedures."

Claudia looked excited enough to burst. Kristy paid close attention to the flight attendant.

I tried hard to pay attention, too, but it was hopeless. I decided that if we crashed, I'd just do whatever Kristy did.

The plane rolled along the ground for awhile, then took off. Connecticut was pitch-black, except for the crisscrossing expressways. Over New York, I felt as if we'd shrunk and were flying around inside the circuit board of some monster computer.

We calmed down somewhere over western Pennsylvania. "What time do you have?" Claudia asked.

"Eight-ten," I replied.

Claudia stared at her watch. "Which is . . . eleven-ten, California time?"

"Five-ten," Kristy corrected her. "We get into L.A. at nine-thirty."

"In the morning?" Claudia asked.

"Nope, the night."

Claudia fiddled with her watch. She looked lost.

Soon dinner was served. We all chose "chicken cordon bleu," which was supposed to be chicken wrapped around ham, with a white sauce.

"Tastes like a tennis ball covered with paste," was Kristy's restaurant review.

"I like it," Claud said with a shrug.

I almost gave her mine. But the flight attendant passed by and smiled at us, and I didn't want to look as if I were insulting her.

Boy, was I grateful for those brownies.

"I can't wait to see Dawn," Claudia said while we were finishing up.

"Me, too," I replied. "It feels like she's been gone for *years*."

"You think she's changed?" Kristy asked.

Claudia laughed. "*You're* worried she picked up bad habits from the We Love Kids Club."

"Hmmph," Kristy replied. "If she has, they won't last long."

"Well, no matter what, she'll still be Dawn," I reminded them.

But I had to admit, I was wondering, too. About a lot of things. How did Dawn feel about her dad's marriage? Would Kristy, Claudia, and I be imposing on their busy house? Would things feel different between Dawn and me? Would she change her mind about coming back to Stoneybrook?

The in-flight movie ended our conversation. It was a comedy about a dog, which we'd all seen but watched again anyway.

During the closing credits, the captain's voice interrupted the soundtrack to tell us we were descending.

Descending? Already?

Kristy, Claudia, and I plastered our faces to the window (well, sort of). For a long time we saw nothing. I began reading a magazine. Then, just as I was about to fall asleep, Kristy screamed, "Look!"

Below us, surrounded by dark hills, was a huge valley of lights. "On behalf of the flight staff, I want to welcome you to Southern California," the captain announced.

"Yeee-*hah*!" Kristy shouted. "Hoo-ray for Hollywood!"

(I love her, but she *can* be embarrassing.)

We fastened our belts. Our landing was a little bumpy. Then we practically had to fight to get into the aisle.

You know what? We were thousands of miles from home, but it didn't feel different at all. I mean, an airport looks like an airport, no matter where you are.

But as we passed through the door, where a grinning flight attendant was saying good-bye, a blast of air came through a narrow opening where the ramp connected to the plane.

Warm air.

That's when it hit me. We were there. Kristy was hopping down the ramp. Claudia was grinning from ear to ear. Me? I was numb. My winter coat felt ridiculous. I felt as if I were in *The Twilight Zone*.

"Hiiiiii!"

There, at the end of the ramp, was Sunshine.

That is Dawn's nickname. It's also a great description of her face when she smiles.

And it also tells you how I felt inside at that moment.

We ran into each other's arms so fast we almost fell over. I had missed her *so much*.

Over her shoulder I could see her dad chatting with Kristy, her dad's fiancée chatting with Claudia, and Jeff looking mildly bored.

"I am so happy you're here!" Dawn cried.

"Me, too," was the only thing I could say before my face turned into Niagara Falls.

CHAPTER 7

Jeff

Palo City, December 16

   Sorry I have not written in the journal yet. I have been very busy.

   Yesterday Mary Anne came with Kristy and Claudia. They are staying here. Tomorrow Dad and Carol get married. I can't wait.

   That's it. Bye now.

Stupid, huh?

Well, I had to write *something*. Dawn would kill me if I didn't.

I tried to be nice. Everybody would get mad at me if I told the truth.

Here's what I should have said: Journals are dumb. I *could* wait till Dad and Carol got married, no problem. And I hate having a house full of girls.

Seriously. I cannot believe how much girls talk. They did not stop from the minute they saw each other at the airport. But first they had to go cry like babies for an hour. You'd think somebody died or something. Everyone in the whole terminal was staring at them.

What did they say to *me*? "Hello," and "You got tall," and "Do you have any girlfriends yet?" (Gag me.) That was it. Nothing else.

Then they turned right back to each other and kept talking. Forget it. They didn't stop in the car. They didn't stop when we went to a late night diner for dessert. They didn't even stop in Dawn's bedroom. That was when it got *worse*! I could hear them right through the walls.

How was a guy supposed to sleep?

If Dawn didn't have to go to school the next morning, they would have talked right through the whole day.

You know what? It was the first time in my life I couldn't wait to go to school.

You know what else? On Christmas Day I'm supposed to fly to Connecticut with Dawn and stay there during Dad's honeymoon. Which means I'll have to listen to all that chattering on two coasts!

I try not to think about it too much.

Anyway, after school Dawn and her friends went to a We ♥ Kids Club meeting together. When I got home, my house was totally quiet. Well, almost. Mrs. Bruen, our housekeeper, was humming to the radio as she cleaned up.

"Hey, what's up, Jeff?" she asked as I walked into the kitchen.

"Nothing."

Mrs. Bruen is cool. She never gets mad, and she laughs at all my jokes. Sometimes she bosses me around, but I don't mind it that much.

I saw the journal, lying on the kitchen table. A note beside it said, WRITE IN THIS IF YOU KNOW WHAT'S GOOD FOR YOU.

"Who wrote that?" I asked.

"I did," Mrs. Bruen said. "I'm tired of your

sister bugging you about it. Make her happy, will you, honey?"

She smiled. I grumbled.

And now you know the real reason I wrote in that dumb thing.

When I finished, Mrs. Bruen was dusting in the living room. "Like the rug?" she asked. "I had it cleaned."

We have this fancy rug — Persian or Moroccan or something — and it had gotten dirty. But now it looked great. "Wow," I said.

To tell you the truth, the whole house looked great. Mrs. Bruen had been working overtime all week.

Why? Because of the wedding. Dad wants the house to look good for guests. He's having a party here afterward.

If you ask me, cleaning up was a ridiculous idea. First of all, it's an *outdoor* party, complete with a tent. Second, parties always leave a mess, so why not clean up *after*? And third, when Carol moves in, the movers are going to drag in all her furniture and stuff, right? That'll get everything even more dusty and dirty.

Sometimes I think kids are way smarter than adults.

I sat down on the couch. I looked around.

We have a wall unit, just across from the couch. I helped Dad put it in. It was so much fun. He kept moving the TV around in it while I sat on the couch, until it was in the perfect place.

Oh, well. Now that would have to be moved, to make room for Carol's wall unit (which is HUMONGOUS). Maybe I'd always have to watch TV on a slant. Maybe the remote wouldn't work at that angle.

Maybe I'd walk around with my head permanently tilted to one side.

Too bad we can't keep the house the way it is. There's just enough stuff in it. What do we need *more* furniture for?

You should see Carol's furniture. It's ugly. She has these things called lava lamps, which look like pig embryos swimming around in colored water tanks. Her couch has an old afghan on it, which covers up all the rips. And her posters are disgusting. All this dumb-looking art with museum names underneath. Most of it is like kindergarten painting.

Plus framed pictures of Mickey Mouse in the bathroom. Even *I'm* too old for that.

"Mrs. Bruen, where is it all going to go?" I asked.

She stopped whistling. "What?"

"Carol's furniture."

"Beats me. Why? You want it all in your room?"

"No *way!*"

Mrs. Bruen was dusting with a feather duster. As she went past me, she did this funny little dance, dusting behind her back, shaking the duster like a tambourine, using it as a microphone.

Sometimes Mrs. Bruen cracks me up.

I got up to go to my room. Halfway there, my stomach kind of clenched up.

Mrs. Bruen. What was going to happen to her?

Dad hired Mrs. Bruen because he's a slob (even *he* admits it). He didn't used to be so bad, but he got much worse after Mom left. Now Carol was moving in. Dad might be neater again. Carol's a good cleaner-upper herself.

We wouldn't need Mrs. Bruen anymore. Which means Dad would have to fire her.

Send her out into the street.

Ruin her whole life.

I would never see her again. And why? All because of Carol. Carol and her pukey furniture.

Why do men have to be *married* anyway? Dad and Mom used to fight all the time. Dad and Carol fight. It doesn't make sense. I mean, if you want to *fight*, you can just do it with your friends. Then you can go home and chill and not have to kiss and make up.

I tried not to think of this stuff. I started reading *My Teacher Is an Alien*, which was scary and funny. That got my mind off everything. But each time I heard Mrs. Bruen, I felt sad again.

Soon I saw Carol's red Miata pull up into the driveway. She and Dad got out, all smiley and laughing. A minute later I heard Mrs. Bruen greet them at the door. She sounded happy, too.

Little did she know she was going to be betrayed.

I heard the thumping of footsteps, then a knock at my door.

"Little pig, little pig, let me in!" Dad said.

Ugh. He has been doing that since I was a baby! Usually I try to rank on him. I say, "Use the chimney," or "I gave at the trough," or something else stupid.

This time I just said, "Yeah."

Dad turned the knob and came in. "Hey, buddy, you all right?"

"Yeah."

"Something happen at school today?"

I shrugged. "No."

"Mrs. Bruen try to air out your sneakers again?"

"No."

Now Carol peeked in behind him. "Hey, Jeffers," she said.

Jeffers? That was new. I didn't like it.

"Hi," I said.

"Something's bugging Jeff," Dad told her. He sat down on the bed next to me. "You sure you don't want to say what it is? Something about the wedding?"

I took a deep breath. I didn't really feel like saying anything. I especially didn't want to talk about Mrs. Bruen when she was close enough to hear.

But I *could* mention the furniture. Dad was being pretty nice. And maybe I was worrying for nothing. Maybe Carol was going to sell her stuff, or give it to a charity, or to the Museum of Modern Ugliness.

"Um, when are the movers coming?" I asked.

Carol rolled her eyes. "The evening of the wedding, if you can imagine *that*."

"Where's all your stuff going to go?" I asked.

She shrugged and looked at Dad. He shrugged, too.

"We haven't thought much about it, to tell you the truth," he said, looking toward his room. "I suppose the dresser will fit in our bedroom."

"It had better," Carol said.

"What about that wall unit?" Dad asked. "We don't really need two."

"True," Carol agreed.

"And I'm sure the Salvation Army will make a pickup at your house on short notice — "

Carol frowned. "*My* house?"

"Well, yeah," Dad replied. "You don't want to keep that thing, do you? I mean, it's not very well made. And you said you've had it since just after college."

"So? It's already a period piece, sweetheart. I came of age with that wall unit. It would be like losing a part of me."

Dad chuckled. "I lose a part of me when I clip my toenails, but — "

"Jack, did I hear you right? Did you say what I thought you said?"

"I was kidding, Carol. But — "

"Besides, your unit is smaller than mine. Maybe you could put it in Jeff's room."

"Yeah!" I blurted out.

Dad gave me a Look. Then he sighed and turned to Carol. "Maybe we should talk about this somewhere else."

They said good-bye. I closed my door.

But I could hear them arguing for the next fifteen minutes or so. While Mrs. Bruen cleaned up around them.

Oh, boy. I had really started something.

CHAPTER 8

Kristy

Palo City, December 16

Hey, California dudes. Take off those shades, put down your surfboards, and let's get to work. Kristy Thomas is here.

Honestly, I don't know how you all do without me....

I was kidding.

Well, *mostly* kidding. The dudes in question were the We ♥ Kids Club. That's what Dawn and a group of baby-sitting friends call themselves.

They have meetings, sort of. They take calls, sort of. And they arrange baby-sitting jobs, sort of. Which makes them a baby-sitters club.

Sort of.

I mean, I don't want to sound rude. They are all great people. They were really nice to me the last time I was in Palo City, and we had fun together. But a club they are not. A club has rules, officers, a dues structure, and regular meetings. A club has *organization*.

Take the Baby-sitters Club. Everyone participates. Jobs are filled. We always have money for whatever we need. Parents trust us to be there when they call.

The We ♥ Kids (So-Called) Club? They meet whenever they feel like it, sometimes at one member's house, sometimes another. No one has a title, and parents can call any member, any time. What happens? Jobs get double-booked and misplaced. And parents still have to call around from sitter to sitter. Which defeats the whole idea of a club in the first place!

Once, the W♥KC was featured in a local

TV newscast. They got a lot of publicity from that — but they were completely overwhelmed. They could not take advantage of it. If that ever happened to the BSC, whoa! We'd be *prepared*.

Thus speaks Chairperson Thomas.

I know, I know. I sound seriously dweeby. All my BSC friends make fun of me for being this way. But if you think about it, it makes sense.

Still don't believe me? Okay, let me tell you about the meeting I went to. It was the day after Claudia, Mary Anne, and I had arrived in California. We had been awake almost the whole night before, gabbing. Then we got up and had a Dawn-style breakfast — wholewheat vegetable pancakes with sprouts. (Yes, I am serious, and no, it did not make me barf.) Claudia, Mary Anne, and I visited Dawn in school for awhile (the school allows that). Afterward, we hung out in the school courtyard with Dawn's best California friend, Sunny Winslow.

Then we heard, "Kristy T.! M.A.! Claudi-o!"

It was Maggie, with brand-new nicknames for us. We all hugged and said hi.

"You look sensational!" Claudia said to Maggie.

She did, too. Her hair was in dreadlocks.

Two of them were dyed red and green. She was wearing this crazy neon-patterned jumpsuit, under a tailored cotton jacket with padded shoulders. I'd never seen anything like it before.

The next thing I knew, Dawn was pulling me toward the front of the school, shouting, "Wait!"

We all ran to the line of school buses. Jill Henderson was starting to climb onto one of them. When she saw us, she jumped back down. "Hi!"

"Hi, Jill!" I exclaimed.

More hugs and kisses, "You look greats," news, gossip, blah blah blah.

Then Sunny suggested a meeting of the We ♥ Kids Club.

"Well, Claudia and Mary Anne and I have to get home and help with the wedding," Dawn explained.

"Just for a few minutes," Sunny insisted. "Then you guys can leave."

"Come on," Maggie pleaded.

"Please please please," Jill said.

Dawn looked at us and shrugged. "Okay."

Boom. The We ♥ Kids Club was about to meet. Just like that. No planning, no nothing.

Kristy, be nice, I told myself. I was not going

to roll my eyes. I was not going to lecture them. I was going to be mature. Accepting.

"Great," was all I said.

Sunny shot me a Look. "Uh-oh," she murmured. Then she cleared her throat and announced, "I hereby move for the official holding of a special meeting."

"I second!" Dawn piped up.

Jill raised her hand. "I third!"

"You *guys*." I couldn't help laughing.

"You know, Kristy," Sunny explained, "we *have* been holding regular meetings lately . . . more or less."

"Uh-huh, that's cool," I replied. Coolly.

I was well-behaved on the walk to Sunny's house, which is in Dawn's neighborhood. When we got there, Dawn, Maggie, and Jill called home to tell their parents where they were.

We watched a video of the W♥KC's TV appearance, then rewound and replayed it again and again. Each time we found something different to laugh about.

Then Sunny said, "Dawn, guess what? Mom got some packs of dried fruit and this fantastic yogurt trail mix."

"Mmm," Dawn yummed.

Ho hum, thought my belly. (The entire We ♥ Kids Club likes health food. I'm sorry, but nuts and dried fruits are not my idea of a snack. Give me Goobers, chocolate pudding, or Triscuits any day.)

"Want to get it, Dawn?" Sunny asked. "It's all in the kitchen cupboards by the fridge."

"Okay," Dawn said.

"And, um, maybe something to drink? Oh. And there's this great fifteen-grain bread — "

"Uh, Sunny, I only have two hands," Dawn said.

Sunny gave a little, high-pitched laugh. "Right. Sorry." She had this wide, plastic grin on her face as Dawn left.

I'd met Sunny before, but I didn't remember her being so strange. Maybe eating all that health food did it to her.

As Dawn went downstairs, Sunny ran to the door and closed it. "Did I sound too obvious?" she whispered.

We looked at her with a group *Duh.*

"Guess what?" Sunny practically squealed. "I've planned a surprise going-away party for her on Sunday!"

"But she's not leaving until next week," I said.

"I know," Sunny replied. "And she'll be too crazy with last-minute stuff. Besides, *you* guys are leaving soon, right? And I want you to be there."

"Cool!" Maggie said.

"Who's coming?" Jill asked.

Sunny rattled off a list of kids she had invited in school. Then she paused. "I think I asked a few others, but I don't remember."

"What time is the party?" Mary Anne asked.

"Oh, I haven't decided yet."

"Our plane flight is that day," I explained.

Sunny's face went blank. "It is? Um, okay. We'll have it early, I guess."

I was beginning to have a sinking feeling about this "party." "Sunny, what kind of plans have you made?"

"Plans?" Sunny repeated.

"Yeah. You know, food and drinks, decorations, activities, stuff like that."

"Oh." Sunny turned kind of pale. "Well, um, I guess I haven't gotten to that."

"This is for Sunday, the *day after tomorrow*?" I asked.

Sunny nodded weakly. "What should I do?"

Hoo, boy.

Thump, thump, thump. We all fell silent at the sound of Dawn's footsteps.

I thought quickly. I knew Dawn, Mary Anne, and Claudia had to leave the meeting

soon. Each of them had stuff to do for the wedding.

But I didn't. I could stay put. And Sunny sure could use my help. No way was she going to be able to pull this off on her own.

Knock-knock-knock. "Room service!" Dawn called out.

Sunny opened the door. Dawn entered with a huge tray, loaded with, well, very *natural-*looking food.

Everyone ate but me. I was too busy thinking.

When they were done, Dawn got up to go. "I think I'll stay and hang out," I said nonchalantly.

Dawn gave me an odd look. "Okay, if you want."

"Watch out," Claudia remarked. "In half an hour, you'll have rules and officers."

"Maybe even a uniform," Dawn added.

I threw an empty trail mix bag at them.

They both ran out with Mary Anne, shouting, " 'Bye!"

I waited a moment, then took a deep breath and grabbed a pen and pad from Sunny's desk. "Okay. What's the name of the nearest grocery store?"

"Wally's," Sunny replied.

At the top of the list I wrote BUY AT WAL-

LY'S, then asked, "And what should we have to eat?"

"Mini rice cakes, ranch-flavor!" Jill suggested.

"String cheese with caraway seeds!" Maggie chimed in.

"Tofu dogs in blankets," was Sunny's contribution. "And veggie chips."

Tofu dogs in blankets? Veggie chips?

I was surprised no one suggested a bowl full of seaweed.

Anyway, I asked Sunny to dictate names of guests she'd invited and guests she wanted to invite. I split the list between Maggie, Jill, and Sunny, and asked them to call the guests and give them specific information.

Then, assuming everyone would come, I made a list of food, including appropriate amounts. Then a list of *simple* decorations — a poster, some streamers, and not much else.

Sunny and Maggie volunteered to do the shopping, so I had them arrange a time to do it together. Next I made everyone decide on a time for the party (ten-thirty A.M.), and Sunny promised to clear it with her parents.

We got so much done in such a short time that the We ♥ Kids Club was practically breathless.

"Kristy, this is fantastic!" Sunny said.

"What a great party!" Maggie added.

Jill was already tapping out a number on the phone.

Me? I was feeling pretty good.

Just call me Kristy the Miracle Worker.

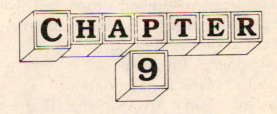

CHAPTER 9

Claudia

Pallo City, Desember 16
Well Kristy, your not the only persin
working hard. Today the Claudia Kishi
weding servise was in high gere. I think
I may have found my true calling!

Lyle, the florist, was thinking. He gazed at the cases of refrigerated flowers before him. The shop smelled so good I thought I would die of delight. Finally he smiled and turned to me. "Nasturtiums," he said.

"Gesundheit," I replied.

He looked blank for a minute.

I blushed. "Sorry. I was joking. That word you said — it sort of sounds like a sneeze . . ."

"Oh." Lyle grinned. "Well, it's the name of a flower. A little expensive, perhaps, but for a wedding these days? *De rigueur.*"

"Okay, then I'll take some of them, instead."

Now he looked confused. "Which?"

"*De rigueurs.*"

"Uh, that's a French word for 'customary.' "

"I meant nasturtiums," I quickly added.

"Mm-hm. All right." He began scribbling on a pad. "And for the best man's lapel, may I suggest stephanotis?"

"Sure." I looked around. "Where is he?"

Lyle glared at me over his glasses. His eyebrows were raised *way* up. That was when I realized Stephan Otis was —

"Another flower, Ms. Kishi," Lyle muttered.

Ugh. I was really blowing it.

You may be wondering what I was doing in a flower shop. Good question. I was working.

Yes, I, Claudia Kishi, was employed in Palo City. I had gone straight to the florist after the We ♥ Kids Club meeting. My boss had ordered flowers in advance, and I was to make sure they looked nice and arrived on time. For my job, I wasn't getting a paycheck.

I was working off my plane ticket.

Confused? Okay, I'll start from the beginning.

Back in Stoneybrook, when Dawn called and asked me to come out West for the wedding, I, of course, said yes.

Unfortunately, I said that before talking to my mom and dad. Dad nodded solemnly and asked how much it cost to fly there. I had no idea. So I got a newspaper and we all looked for airline ads.

Do you know the signs of severe shock? Popping eyes, a sudden gasp, and dead silence. I discovered this when Dad found a list of plane fares in the *Stoneybrook News*.

Hasta la vista, L.A. Or so I thought.

I didn't give up easily. I pleaded. I cajoled (I'm not sure what that means, but I must have done it). But Dad was firm. Too many expenses — my sister's college courses (she's in high school but she's a certified genius), my art lessons and supplies, et cetera, et cetera.

Oooh, was I mad.

I stormed up to my room, called Dawn, and broke the bad news. She was sad. She said that she understood, and that they'd all miss me.

When I hung up, I crawled under my blankets and vowed never to get up. *Never.* Not if the earth opened up. Not if an atom bomb dropped on my front yard or a typhoon blew off my roof.

Rrrrriinggg!

The phone! I hopped out of bed and grabbed it.

" 'lo," I grumbled.

"Claudia, it's Dawn. Guess what? Dad says he needs your artistic talents."

I exhaled loudly. "Dawn, you don't know my parents. When they say no, they mean — "

"No, no, you don't understand!" Dawn interrupted. "He wants to *hire* you."

"Huh?"

"To be, like, a wedding consultant. You'd

be in charge of picking the flowers, decorating the house, maybe even styling hair."

"What? I've never done — "

"Claud, you would be great at that, and you know it!"

"I guess, but — "

"Look, we're *all* helping out, Claudia. That's the kind of wedding Dad and Carol want — with friends and family involved, instead of hiring a lot of strangers."

"I don't know. . . . I mean, what would I charge?"

"Dad figured that out. He's willing to pay exactly half the cost of a round-trip plane ticket. Plus you can stay at my house. You and Kristy can sleep in the living room."

What a deal! I was stunned. I mean, just to be *asked* was a real honor. At least I thought so.

I said good-bye, ran downstairs, and asked my parents. Dad wasn't so hot on the idea. He thought the whole thing would make him look bad, like he couldn't afford the ticket. But I insisted Mr. Schafer was going to be getting a good bargain (which, I thought, was true).

We settled on a compromise. Dad and Mom would charge the ticket on their credit card. I would earn the money, but only after I did the work. Then I would use that money to pay my parents back.

And that is how I became Claudia Kishi, Wedding Consultant!

Ta-da!

Back to Lyle.

"So let's see," he said, shoving his glasses up the length of his nose, "I'll have the bouquet for the bride, a smaller bouquet for the bridesmaid, a boutonniere for the best man, four centerpieces, garlands for the house and tent. Anything else?"

"Oh!" I had almost forgotten what Mr. Schafer had asked me when he'd dropped me off. "Could you bring a Christmas tree?"

Lyle scratched his head. "Well, we are affiliated with a local nursery. I suppose we could."

"Great. Thanks!"

Lyle added up the bill. He showed it to me and I nodded. (Did I *see* the amount? Noooo.)

As he walked me to the door, he had this big smile. I think he was happy to get rid of me.

I took one last, deep sniff and said goodbye.

Next stop, The Current Affair. That's a catering company that has a small gourmet shop in the Vista Hills mall. Mr. Schafer and Carol had called them to arrange a buffet-style dinner at their house after the wedding. My job was to give them some of Carol's last-minute requests.

"Hi," I said to a harried-looking man in the shop. "I'm here about the Schafer-Olson wedding."

"Hello! I'm Stuart." He was all smiles now. "What can I do for you?"

I read from the list Carol had given me:

"Stuffed grape leaves, unsweetened yams for a man who's a diabetic, roast duck instead of turkey, and carrot cake instead of a white cake."

When I looked up, Smiling Stuart had turned into The Monster from the Mall. He was glaring at me. "Uh, tell me who you are again?"

"Claudia Kishi? Dawn — the groom's daughter — is my friend. I'm visiting from Connecticut."

"A friend," he repeated. "And you're in the wedding?"

"*In* it? No."

I could swear I saw steam coming out of his ears. He turned to a desk and flipped through a Rolodex. "Let me call Mr. Schafer."

He did. And boy, he was *much* more polite to him than he was to me. But even so, I could see his face grow grimmer.

After he hung up, he took my list and said, "All right, Ms. Keithly, I'll do what I can."

"Kishi," I reminded him as I left.

(No, he did not say, "*Gesundheit.*")

I had one more stop: Carswell-Hayes, to buy sunglasses (for Kristy, Mary Anne, and me), and suntan lotion (for everyone). Yes, we'd forgotten to pack that stuff. Who thinks about all that in the middle of a Connecticut winter? Anyway, the wedding was going to be held on a beach, so we all needed protection.

A wedding on the beach! I could hardly think of anything more romantic. The sun beating down. The waves crashing in the background, the wind blowing our hair.

Hmmmm . . .

As I walked across the mall, I pulled a pen out of my shoulder bag. I scribbled EXTRA HAIRSPRAY on my list of wedding things to buy.

CHAPTER 10

Mary Anne

Palo City, December 16

A beach wedding. Wow. Before this trip, I'd never heard of such a thing. It ought to be really interesting!

So far the trip has been great. I love California, even though I feel kind of dreamy and tired all the time. Jet lag, I guess (or maybe it was all the talking last night).

Sorry, Dawn, but I don't know if I could ever get used to living here. Nine days till Christmas and it's 73 degrees outside. On our walk to Sunny's house, I saw a Santa Claus in sandals and red shorts.

Is there such a thing as season lag? I think that's what I have.

Anyway, Dawn and I have just returned from Sunny's house. Dawn is upstairs now, and she says she wants to surprise me. It's something about the wedding....

"One more minute!" Dawn called from her bedroom.

"Okay!" I replied.

I closed my journal and waited.

Did I sound too unexcited about the beach wedding? I hope not. I tried to be positive.

But I have to admit, the idea sounded a little strange to me. I know, I know, it *shouldn't.* Beaches are fun. Romantic.

They're also sandy and windy. And if I'm not totally covered from head to toe, and wearing a floppy hat, I end up looking like a carrot with hair.

Besides, I guess I was expecting a normal wedding. At a church. With organ music and a white dress with a veil and a groom waiting by the altar, beaming at his true love's approach as everyone sniffles happily.

I adore church weddings. At my dad's, I cried and cried. I will never forget it. I was kind of looking forward to one just like it.

Where do you *sit* at a beach wedding? Are you supposed to stand the whole time? What if sand gets in your shoes? Or do you go barefoot under your nicest outfit, holding your shoes in one hand?

More questions: How can you see the bride if you're squinting in the sun and the wind is blowing your hair around? What do you do if surfers and tourists start gawking? And what about the music? Does someone bring an accordion? A harmonica?

I wouldn't dare say any of this to Dawn. She seemed thrilled about the idea. And after all, it's *her* dad. I was determined to be a good guest.

"Da dum de dum . . . da dum de dum. . . ." Dawn da-dummed the wedding song as she descended.

"Wowww . . ."

Dawn looked gorgeous. She was wearing a satiny, bare-shoulder dress I'd never seen before.

"Like it?" she said at the bottom of the stairs, turning around.

"Stunning! Is that what you're wearing at the wedding?"

Dawn looked at me a little oddly. "Yeah, but — "

"Can I show you the dress I brought?" I asked, getting up from the kitchen table.

But as I tried to go upstairs, Dawn said, "Mary Anne, this is the bridesmaids' dress."

"Yes, I know — "

"I — I bought one for you, too."

I was at the top step. I turned around. "For *me*?"

"Bridesmaids always wear matching dresses, Mary Anne." Dawn lowered her head sheepishly. "You don't like it, do you? Oh, I knew I should have asked you about it beforehand."

"*Bridesmaid?*" I managed to squeak. "I'm a bridesmaid?"

"Well, yeah. Didn't we talk about it?"

"Dawn, you told me *you* were a bridesmaid. You didn't tell me *I* had to be one."

"Oops." Dawn's face turned red as I walked back downstairs. "Sorry. I guess I just assumed you knew. Are you mad at me?"

"Well, no, not *mad* . . ." *Panicked* was more like it. I plopped into a kitchen chair. "What will I have to do?"

"Hardly anything," Dawn replied. "You walk in before the bride and groom, smile, and look radiant and luminous."

"In front of all those people?"

"Only about forty."

"*Forty?* And we have to stand there, facing them throughout the whole ceremony?"

Dawn laughed. "Mary Anne, it's not like you have to recite a poem or twirl a baton. Don't worry." She looked upstairs, all excited. "Hey, you want to try on your dress?"

"I guess."

I tried to smile. I followed Dawn to her room. She took the dress out of the closet. I tried it on.

All the time I was trying not to cry. Or scream.

I am a very quiet person. I *hate* confrontation. But you know what I hate worse? Being the center of attention. Knowing that people are staring at me.

"It fits!" Dawn exclaimed as she zipped me up the back. "You look sensational!"

It was a nice dress. Nice, bright, and slinky. Perfect for Dawn.

But not for *me*. I hated the way my shoulders looked. Like big, white, slabs of beef. How was I going to cover them against the sun? An umbrella? Shoulder pads? A beach blanket?

"Well? What do you think?" Dawn asked.

"Um, nice." I couldn't wait to take it off. I began pulling the shoulders down.

"What's wrong, Mary Anne?" Dawn asked.

"Nothing," I lied.

"Hey, I'm your sister. Remember? Talk to me."

I stepped out of the dress and quickly put my clothes back on. "It's just that . . . well, I had a whole different idea about this wedding."

Dawn looked exasperated. "Mary Anne, I don't understand you. You love weddings."

"But no one told me I'd have to be *in* one."

"It's an honor, Mary Anne!" Dawn's voice was getting louder. "Any other girl would be thrilled!"

"Well, I'm shy in front of people. You know that."

Dawn threw up her arms. "Everyone'll be looking at the bride and groom! No one's going to care about *you*. They won't even know you're there."

"Oh, thanks a lot."

"I didn't mean it the way it sounded."

"*Everyone* will be looking at me, Dawn. Because I'll be the only one wearing a big hat and a towel over my sunburned shoulders."

"Is that what you're worried about?"

"Well, that's another thing no one told me. I didn't know about this beach stuff. I thought the wedding was going to be, you know, *normal*."

Dawn's eyes grew buggy. "Oh, so we're abnormal now. The truth comes out. You're embarrassed!"

We fell silent. Dawn stared out the window. I fiddled with the laces on my sneakers. I was *not* going to start crying.

When I looked at Dawn, I could see tears in *her* eyes. Suddenly the argument seemed pretty dumb.

"I didn't mean that, Dawn," I said. "I'm sorry."

Dawn nodded. "Yeah. It's okay. I'm the one who really blew it."

"No, I was too sensitive."

"I was too stupid."

We both stopped. I felt a tear trickling down my cheek. Dawn started crying and laughing at the same time. I opened my arms.

We were about to hug when Dawn said, "Aaaugh! Get away! No tear stains on the new dress!"

We burst out giggling. I heard a door opening down the hall, then footsteps. "Will you two knock it off?" Jeff's voice roared.

"Sorry!" I replied.

Smiling, I picked up my dress and hung it back up. Dawn changed into her casual clothes.

I felt like a fool. Dawn was right, it was an honor to be a bridesmaid. Besides, everyone makes mistakes. Dawn had been busy, and she forgot to tell me I was going to be in the wedding. That's all. I shouldn't have been so hard on her.

I was going to get over my shyness. And be the best bridesmaid I could be.

Beach or no beach.

Dawn and I were friends again. (Yea!) When the front doorbell rang, we raced each other downstairs, giggling all the way.

Both of us grabbed the doorknob and yanked it open.

"When's dinner? I'm starving!"

Can you tell who it was? If you guessed Kristy, you were right.

"Didn't you eat at Sunny's?" Dawn asked.

"I tried a piece of that bread, but it was like eating wood. I can't wait for some real food."

Dawn put her hands on her hips. But before she could answer, Carol's car pulled up in front of the house.

"Who wants to help bring in some takeout food?" Carol shouted from the driver's window.

We ran outside. Mr. Schafer was already out of the car, heading straight for the trunk. Claudia climbed out behind him, looking tired and gloomy.

"Smells yummy," Dawn said, grabbing a bag out of the trunk. "Where'd you get the food?"

"This new restaurant, Body-Soul Joy," Mr. Schafer replied. "It's macrobiotic."

"Macro who?" Kristy asked, reaching for a bag.

Dawn rolled her eyes. "It's food that puts your body in harmony with nature. You know, whole grains, no animal foods except fish, no salt or sugar, all natural flavors."

No wonder Claudia looked sick.

Kristy's hand froze on the way to her bag.

Instead of lifting it out, she peered warily inside. Her nose crinkled. I could see visions of cheeseburgers dancing in her head.

Inside the house, Dawn merrily set the food out. "Mmm, flounder with ginger-burdock root sauce . . . millet croquettes . . . seitan patties . . . veggie-gluten pizza . . . and mu tea! I love mu tea!"

I thought Kristy was going to throw up right there. *"Moo tea?"* she said. "What's it made from? Boiled cow ears?"

"Ewww, *Kristy!*" Claudia said, trying not to crack up.

We joked about the food all through dinner. And you know what? The stuff tasted pretty good, if you pretended you didn't know what it was. (Even Kristy gorged herself.)

Afterward, Mr. Schafer said, "Okay, let's clear out the living room and have a short wedding rehearsal."

We put the coffee table on the couch, making lots of floor space.

"Okay," Carol said. "It's going to be pretty informal. Charida, my friend from work, will stop by here and drive you girls to the beach a little early. At the beginning, you can just mingle. Jack and I will arrive later, with our maid of honor." (She smiled at Dawn.) "And our best man, Jeffers."

Maid of honor? That made me the only regular bridesmaid. I gulped. *Easy, Mary Anne*, I said to myself.

"Kristy, you'll be in charge of getting the guests to make an aisle in the middle when you see us pull up," Mr. Schafer explained. "Reverend Gunness, our celebrant, will take her place at the end of the aisle. Then the four of us in the wedding party will leave the car and walk — "

"Four?" Dawn interrupted. "What about the bridesmaids and ushers?"

Mr. Schafer looked at her blankly, then chuckled. "Not at this kind of wedding, Sunshine. Maybe the next one."

"Next one?" Carol glowered at him.

"Kidding!" Mr. Schafer shot back.

"Oooh," Claudia said with a smile.

"Hit him with a millet croquette!" Kristy suggested.

Everyone laughed, except Dawn and me.

I was in shock. What was going on? First I wasn't a bridesmaid. Then I was. Now I wasn't again.

Had Dawn made her plans without even talking to her dad? How could she do that to me?

To tell you the truth, now I'd kind of gotten used to the idea. It would have been fun —

standing up there with my sister, sharing her special day.

Didn't I deserve to be a bridesmaid? Why *hadn't* Mr. Schafer asked me?

Dawn was giving me this wounded puppy-dog look. But every time I glanced her way, I saw red. I have never been so angry.

I don't remember much about the rest of the evening. Later that night, Dawn came into the bathroom while I was brushing my teeth.

She shut the door and sighed. "Boy, did I blow it."

I had a toothbrush in my mouth. I said nothing.

"Well, now you don't have to worry about your shoulders," she continued, smiling, "or about being in front of a crowd."

I rinsed and spat. "Dawn, you never asked your dad about me being a bridesmaid?"

"I guess not," Dawn replied. "I — I admit, I've been a real airhead. Are you angry?"

"Well, how would you feel? I mean, I am your sister. Doesn't your dad like me?"

"Wait a minute. You said you didn't *want* to be in the wedding!"

"That was before you told me about it!" I shot back. "Then I planned on it. Now it turns out no one cared about me in the first place."

110

Dawn stormed away, shaking her head. "Mary Anne, I will never understand you!"

"I know! You already proved it!"

I couldn't believe I'd said that. Taking my toothbrush, I ran downstairs.

I was able to reach the living room couch before I burst into tears.

CHAPTER 11

Jessi

Stoneybrook, December 17
This is it! The
big wedding day!
Well, for everyone
else. Not for me.
I am going
to spend the
day in Bellair's.
Today I make
my debut as Santa....

I almost didn't show up. I woke up that morning with cold feet.

No, my covers had not fallen off. I was *scared*.

The kids were going to laugh at me. Pull my beard off. Or worse, they'd burst out crying. They'd be disappointed. *Traumatized*.

Come to Bellair's and see the Incredible Shrinking Santa!

Why did the store have to have a Santa? And who ever made up this stupid legend anyway?

Bah, humbug.

When I went downstairs, Daddy was serving up scrambled eggs and hash browns for breakfast. Mama was making orange juice, and Aunt Cecelia was bustling around setting the table. My sister, Becca, was feeding the baby in his high chair. "The baby" is my brother, Squirt, who is actually a year and a half. (Becca is eight.)

Now, I love big breakfasts. My ballet teacher, Mme Noelle, would faint if she knew this. As a ballerina, I'm supposed to watch my weight. "No one wants to watch zee doncing heepos, except in *Fantasia!*" she likes to say.

But I don't get too crazy about my weight (yet). I will someday, when I'm a pro. On

Saturday mornings I eat like a pig. And I enjoy every minute of it.

That Saturday morning was different. I might as well have had sawdust on my plate.

"Aren't you eating anything?" asked my mom.

I pushed some of my hash browns into a mound. "I'm not that hungry."

"Huh-gee!" chirped Squirt. He flung a slice of banana on the floor.

"I'll eat it!" Becca volunteered.

"Don't you touch that banana!" Aunt Cecelia bellowed.

"Not *that*!" Becca said. "Jessi's breakfast."

As Becca scooped my eggs and potatoes onto her plate, Aunt Cecelia shook her head. "When I was your age, Jessica Ramsey, I would have been grateful for a breakfast like that."

"When you were her age," Daddy said, "you must have been *full* of gratitude, Cecelia. Because half the time you stole my breakfast, too."

"She *did*?" Becca asked, her eyes lighting up.

"Well, I never — " Aunt Cecelia sputtered.

"That's what stunted my growth," Daddy went on. (Daddy, by the way, is six feet two and two hundred pounds.)

Aunt Cecelia huffed and puffed and turned away, but I could see her smiling.

Daddy is the only one brave enough to tease Aunt Cecelia. They're brother and sister. (She came to live with us when Mama went back to work.)

"Just one bite before you go?" Mama asked.

I looked at the clock: 9:09. I was supposed to be at Bellair's by ten at the latest.

"No, thanks. I better leave," I said, bolting upward.

"Jessi is going to be a Santa Claus," Becca announced to Squirt.

"San-toss! San-toss!" Squirt began banging his high chair tray. Apple juice sprayed all over the place. Becca started giggling. Aunt Cecelia screamed. Mama hit the floor with a sponge.

"Sorry to leave you in this time of crisis," Daddy said, grabbing his coat.

We were out the door before we heard Mama's response.

Leave it to Daddy. He can make me laugh when I'm feeling awful.

All the way to the store, he kept telling me how great I was going to be. I tried to believe it. I tried and tried. In the mall parking lot, I bravely got out, said good-bye, and walked toward the employees' entrance.

But when I saw Ms. Javorsky waiting there, I nearly dove back into the car. I think I would have, if she hadn't spotted me.

"Ah, what to my wondering eyes should appear, but jolly Saint Nick and her charioteer!" Ms. Javorsky called out.

I could hear Daddy laughing as he drove out of sight.

Me? I tried to laugh, too. But what came out was this sound halfway between a chuckle and a nose blow.

"How are feeling?" Ms. Javorsky asked.

"Fine," I replied.

"Ready for a huge crowd? This is one of the big shopping days before Christmas."

"Yeah."

Ha. What a fib. But what could I say? "Please keep the kids away from me"?

Ms. Javorsky led me into the employee locker room. A few women were freshening up, but none of them seemed to notice me. No one pointed or shook her head. I guess Ms. Javorsky hadn't told them about me.

She opened up a locker. Inside was my costume. "Come see me in my office before you go out on the floor," she said, walking away.

I stared at the big, gaudy outfit. For a teeny

moment I thought of burning it. But I didn't. I put it on — stomach padding, white beard, hat, and all. I took my bell.

I thought I would die on the way to Ms. Javorsky's office. I felt the posters on the wall laughing at me. She insisted I looked great and brought me out onto "the floor."

It was still pretty early. I had come out into the housewares section, so most of the shoppers were adults.

I hung out by the coffee grinders. I memorized all the sale prices. Once in awhile, when no one was around, I rang my bell.

Yawn. Boy, did that get boring fast.

From where I was standing, I could see the toy department at the opposite end of the floor. I could hear it, too. Kids were yelling, squealing, bugging their parents.

At the entrance to the department, a small crowd had formed. A bunch of kids were sitting in front of a temporary-looking stage. Across the stage was a curtain.

I walked closer. Soon I could make out a sign that said SILLY SIMON THE CLOWN 10:15, 11:15, 12:15, 1:15.

"Santa! Santa!" a voice piped up.

Every single face in the crowd turned my way. I was caught.

"Ho ho ho!"

I sounded like . . . like a scared girl. I waited for them to shriek with laughter. Hold their noses. Throw wadded-up gift wrap. Silly Simon was going to emerge and bonk me over the head with a rubber chicken.

Then I felt a tug at my jacket. I looked to my left and saw a little girl staring up at me.

"Hi," she said.

I tried to deepen my voice. "Hello, there."

"Can I get a brother?" she asked.

Huh?

My very first kid, and does she ask for a Barbie? A truck? A video?

No. A real, live human being.

I looked at her mom. She was all smiles. She was also *very* pregnant.

"Oh! A *brother*! Well, um, you know, sisters are nice, too."

"No, no, *no*! She'll play with my toys. I hate sisters."

I laughed. "I know how you feel. How old are you?"

She held up four fingers and a bent thumb.

"Well, when your sister or brother is four and a half, you know how old you'll be?"

"Uh-uh."

"Nine."

Her eyes lit up. "Wow! I'll be this tall." She raised her hands high over her head.

"Do you think you'll want to play with the toys you have now?"

"No *way*, silly." She thought for a moment. "I'll be growed up."

I made a sad face. "Then what will happen to your poor, lonely toys?"

"I can give them to a *little* girl," she said, as if it were the most obvious thing in the world. "Like if I have a sister."

"Ho ho ho! Great idea!"

" 'Bye!"

Her mom winked at me as the girl pulled her away. "How did you know?" she whispered, patting her tummy.

Boy, was I proud of myself. I guess my BSC training came in handy.

I rang my bell loudly. "Ho ho ho!"

A boy looked up at me through narrow eyes. "I know you're not really Santa."

Gulp.

"Merry Christmas!" was my lame reply.

"You're a *helper*," he announced.

"Thimbles and thunderstorms!" I replied. "How did you know?"

The boy giggled. Then he gave me a folded-

up note. "Could you please give this to your boss?"

"You bet!"

"Thanks! 'Bye!"

Thimbles and thunderstorms? That was an expression I'd read in one of the Chronicles of Narnia books. I couldn't believe it had popped into my head.

I was on a roll. One shy little African-American boy stayed glued to my side for about five minutes, just smiling silently. A girl in an expensive party outfit told me she wanted a real horse, but would settle for a motorcycle. A pair of twins argued over who had been "better" during the year. One boy gave me a brochure with a cover labeled *Oliver's Wish List* in complex computer graphics. (Inside was an illustrated catalog of gifts.) At one point, Silly Simon brought me onstage in the middle of his show and pulled a red scarf out of my ear.

You know what? When Ms. Javorsky came over to tell me my shift had ended, I begged her to let me stay on awhile longer.

"Are you sure you want to?" she asked. "It's been over four hours."

"Just another half hour or so," I said. "Please? I'll call home to let my parents know."

"All right," Ms. Javorsky said with a chuckle. "Then make sure you go home and get some rest."

"Thanks!"

Get some rest? Who needed rest? I could have stayed there till midnight.

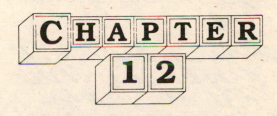

CHAPTER 12

Mary Anne

Palo City, December 17
The Day!

It is now almost nine o'clock. In one hour, Dawn will have a new stepmother.

You should see the house. Mrs. Bruen is running around like crazy. I walked from the living room to the den, and she was in both places. I don't know how she did it.

Mary Anne

Claudia's helping
Dawn with her flowers.
They're making up
a song:

Here comes the bride,
all dressed in white
After the beach,
go buy some bleach,
'Cause every dress
will be such a mess....

Dawn can be very creative. When she's not being forgetful and inconsiderate.

On Friday night, after the big argument, I ended up watching TV in the living room with Claudia and Kristy. By the time I got back upstairs, Dawn was fast asleep. I crawled into my sleeping bag without a word.

When I awoke the next morning, Dawn was sitting up in her bed.

My first urge was to say good morning. That urge lasted about five seconds. All the memories of our fight came flooding back.

"Don't hate me," were Dawn's first words.

I looked at the floor. I played with the zipper of my sleeping bag. Finally I replied, "I don't."

"I'm sorry, Mary Anne. Really. I assumed so much. I should have realized what a big deal this was. I should have talked over everything with Carol and Dad. Somehow I figured I was, like, automatically in charge of the bridesmaids." She sighed. "I was so excited about you and me sharing this together. I got all spacey."

I listened closely. I tried to swallow the lump that was forming in my throat.

You know what picture popped into my mind? Sunglasses in an oatmeal cannister in our house in Stoneybrook. Sharon had left them there. Dawn's mom. I thought about the ways my dad and I are alike — both super-organized and quiet and serious. Dawn was like her mom, too, in some ways. It was only natural.

It didn't make what she did less hurtful. I mean, leaving sunglasses wasn't the same as messing up wedding arrangements. But thinking about that connection made me feel less angry.

"It's all right, Dawn," I said softly. "I'm sorry I was so negative about the wedding being on the beach and all. And I really do like the dress."

"Oh, you don't have to worry about that. The saleswoman said I could take it back — "

"Actually, I thought I might wear it," I said. "My dress isn't really . . . beachy."

"Oh, you won't be sorry! You know, the sun isn't that strong this time of year. And Claudia bought some sunblock, just in case. SPF 30, I think."

"You don't mind?" I asked. "Won't people be confused if I'm wearing the same dress as a bridesmaid?"

Dawn shrugged. "Tough. We're sisters. We can dress alike if we want."

Would it bore you to know Dawn and I hugged and cried *again*? Well, we did.

Sigh. It's been that kind of trip.

Anyway, I was glad we got the bad stuff out of our systems so early, while the house was quiet. A minute later Mr. Schafer's voice trumpeted out: "Rise and shine! Big day ahead! Eat breakfast now or forever hold your peace!"

Before I could fold up my sleeping bag, a truck screeched to a stop in front of the house. We watched out Dawn's window as a team of workers unloaded tables, chairs, and a folded-up tent.

Then Claudia and Kristy came barreling upstairs. They had been sleeping in the living room and were still in their pj's.

"Aaaaah!" Claudia screamed. "It's a group Bad Hair Day!"

It was true. Let me tell you, looking in the mirror is not great for your self-esteem after a night in a sleeping bag. My hair looked like shredded wheat. "Oh, noooo," I moaned.

"Have no fear," Claudia continued. "Everybody take a shower, get dressed, and report to the Kishi hair clinic — on the double!"

"Yes, ma'am!" Dawn replied.

Kristy smiled at Claud with admiration. "You sound like me."

I got the upstairs shower, and Dawn the downstairs one. We came rushing back into the bedroom at the same time. We threw on some old clothes and flew down to the kitchen. Mrs. Bruen was already there, flipping pancakes while Jeff set a huge, steaming stack of them on the table.

Claudia and Kristy had showered and dressed casually by that time, too. The four of us stood there in the kitchen, hair all wet and tangled, just gawking at those pancakes.

"Help yourself," Mrs. Bruen said.

Forget the hair. We were *starving*. We sat at the table and shoveled the food in.

Mr. Schafer whisked in, wearing his undershirt and a beautiful pair of linen pants. "Well,

well! It's breakfast with Medusa and the Gorgons."

"Ha ha," Dawn said.

"What's that, a rock group?" Claudia asked.

"No, it's these women from a Greek myth who have snakes instead of hair," Dawn replied.

Jeff burst out laughing.

"It was a joke," Mr. Schafer said. "You all look sensational."

"Just you wait." Claudia stood up. "Guys, let's get started."

She rushed us into the bathroom and began her . . . art.

Luckily Kristy was first. When Claudia tried to give her the finger-in-the-electric-socket punk look, Kristy blew up.

Afterward, Claud became a lot more conservative. She worked the kinks out of my hair and moussed it just enough to give it some shine and body. She hot-curled a wave into Dawn's hair, then gathered some from the sides with these gorgeous silk-flower combs she'd bought.

As we were watching her work on Dawn, the doorbell rang. Jeff yelled out, "It's the ups truck!"

"U.P.S.," Mr. Schafer corrected him from upstairs. "Have Mrs. Bruen sign for it."

A few minutes later we heard rumbling and grunting and thudding from the back door area. Kristy and I ran into the kitchen to see two men dumping box after box onto the floor of the outer hallway.

Mrs. Bruen looked horrified. Mr. Schafer was grinning.

"A wedding and Christmas at the same time," Mr. Schafer said. "What a life!"

"Where are we going to put all this stuff?" Mrs. Bruen asked, shaking her head.

"No! No! Farther from the garage!" Mr. Schafer barged out the back door, yelling at the tent people.

The minute Dawn stepped out the door, Claudia cried, "Uh, uh! Not till you get sprayed. I don't want my work ruined."

We scampered back to the bathroom. Mrs. Bruen was now chasing Jeff around, holding out a suit in a dry cleaning bag. "Jeffrey, your father wants you to put this on."

"No one wears a *suit* to the beach!" Jeff protested.

"Your father is wearing one," Mrs. Bruen said.

"He's getting married."

"And *you're* the best man."

"So? That doesn't mean I have to look stupid."

Tsssssssssssss . . . The sound of the hairspray drowned out our giggling.

Next Dawn and I ran back upstairs. We grabbed our dresses out of the closet and put them on.

Funny. Mine felt way too big. Had I lost weight since the day before?

I considered wearing my own dress until I looked at Dawn. Her dress came up to her knees.

"*Gaaack*," she muttered.

We exploded with laughter. Then we switched dresses.

Claudia barged into the room with a gorgeous corsage for Dawn.

"Which side am I supposed to wear it on?" Dawn asked.

They talked and fussed. Quickly I grabbed my journal and wrote in it.

Finally Mrs. Bruen called up, "We're leaving in five minutes!"

We rushed downstairs. Claudia ran around fixing everybody's hair. Mrs. Bruen ran around with a necktie, chasing Jeff. Mr. Schafer ran around giving last minute instructions to all the workers. Now caterers were in the kitchen, running around with huge trays of food.

Dawn and I had nothing to do. So we ran

around, too — to keep from going crazy.

Phweeeeeeet!

A familiar whistle sounded in the living room. "Everyone into the car!" Kristy shouted.

Yes, President Kristy had brought her coach's whistle all the way from Connecticut.

Dawn and I hugged each other good-bye. Claudia, Kristy, Mrs. Bruen, and I ran out to the car.

Mrs. Bruen started it up. I held my breath and squeezed Kristy's hand.

We were on our way.

CHAPTER 13

Dawn

Palo City, December 17
   My father was married today.
   He was dressed in a linen jacket, and he looked like a movie star. Carol, ~~his fiancee~~ my stepmother, wore a flowing Indian-print dress that shim-mered in the breeze. I think this was the first time I'd seen her in makeup. She was soooo gorgeous.

*Now both my parents
are married again. I
feel proud of them.
Isn't that weird? It's
like I'm the parent and
they're my kids.
Funny what this
wedding is doing to me....*

"Easy on the gas, sweetheart."

Carol was being very patient with my dad. He was driving like a maniac.

He's bad enough, normally. But on his wedding day, I guess the road was not the first thing on his mind.

I was sitting in the backseat. Next to me, Jeff was squirming, knotting and unknotting his tie.

"Turn left here, dear," Carol said to Dad.

Screeeeek!

Dad turned all right. Too bad he hadn't done it more slowly.

"Who-o-o-oa!" Jeff cried out, falling backward over my lap.

Dad stabilized the car. A horn blared outside. I gently pushed Jeff back up. He went back to work on his tie. Carol was biting her nails.

Strange. Looking at the front seat of the car,

seeing the backs of two heads, I kept thinking of Mom.

I have a picture in my mind, from years and years of riding in the back of this same car — and in that picture, Mom is always the person next to Dad. I see them singing, joking, leading us in car games. At least, that's what I remember when I was a little girl.

But I also remember the later rides, when I was older. Mom and Dad would try to be all nice and cheerful around Jeff and me, but they'd hardly say a word to each other. When they were looking forward, their faces were like stone.

After the divorce, it was hard to picture my parents married to other people. I adjusted to Mom's remarriage, because I adored Mary Anne and her dad. But as for *my* dad? Well, for a long time I wasn't sure I liked Carol. She can go overboard, trying to seem young and cool. Not long after I came to California, she and Dad broke up. I think Carol was jealous of the attention Dad was giving me.

I'd been jealous, too. Part of me was glad they split.

But part of me missed Carol. And now, seeing the two of them on the drive to the beach, I knew why.

Dad was like his old self. (Except for the

nervousness. But I think getting married is a good excuse for that.) I could tell he was happy. I could see the way his eyes would dart over to Carol. And I could see how he relaxed when she put her arm around him.

I was happy. Dad was doing the right thing.

Believe it or not, he got us to the beach in one piece. Someone had cordoned off a bunch of parking spaces with traffic cones and blue-and-white crepe paper.

In the center of the line of cars, near a large crowd of dressed-up people, was a huge space.

Claudia, Maggie, and Sunny were standing in it. Claud started waving her arms. "Here! Here!"

Dad drove smoothly in. The crowd began moving toward us, but I could see Kristy urging everyone back onto the sand.

She did *not*, however, use her whistle. (Thank goodness.)

Carol's face had changed. Her skin was pale. Her eyes were egg-sized.

"How's my hair?" she asked.

"Beautiful," Dad replied.

"Did I sweat through my makeup?"

"No, sweetheart."

"Where are my flowers?"

Dad lifted them off the seat next to her.

"Right here." He threw us a wink. "How's our bridal party?"

"Fine," I said.

"Do I *have* to wear this tie?" Jeff whined.

Dad chuckled. "After I kiss the bride, you can take it off and throw it in the air."

Jeff's face lit up. "All *riiiiight*!"

"Okay, everybody," Carol said. "Let's go."

I opened my door and stepped out. The air was cool, but the sun seemed pretty strong. I hoped Mary Anne had worn a lot of sunblock. Aside from the wedding guests, not too many people were on the beach (even in California, December isn't always beach weather).

Mary Anne, Claudia, and Kristy had done a great job. The crowd had split in the middle. Just beyond them stood Reverend Gunness, a freckle-faced woman with a crinkly, welcoming grin.

The members of the Baby-sitters Club and the We ♥ Kids Club were hanging around together, all smiles. Off to one side stood a group of Carol's and Dad's friends. One of them started strumming a guitar. The others, who were holding sheets of paper, began to sing:

" '*Tis the gift to be simple, 'tis the gift to be free,*

'Tis the gift to come down where you want to be,
And when we find ourselves in the place just right,
'Twill be in the valley of love and delight. . . ."

Their voices drifted across the beach. The song was so beautiful I almost forgot what I had to do.

"Link arms!" Mrs. Bruen whispered to Jeff and me.

I held out my left arm.

Jeff looked as if I'd handed him a dead fish. "Do we *have* to?"

"Yes!" said all the rest of us.

With a disgusted grunt, he limply took hold of my elbow. Oh, well, we take what we get.

To the sound of the music and the gentle waves, Jeff and I walked up the aisle.

Some of the guests were wearing sunglasses, so I couldn't tell whether they were teary-eyed. But the others couldn't hide it.

I caught a glimpse of Mary Anne. She wasn't teary-eyed. She was past that stage. Water was cascading down her cheeks. If she were any nearer the surf, she'd make the tide rise.

I smiled at her and gave a little wave.

Jeff and I stood on either side of Reverend Gunness, who was beaming.

I turned to face Dad and Carol. They had held back, so they could proceed down the "aisle" by themselves.

They began walking, slowly. They held hands. Carol pressed her bouquet to her chest. Her dress billowed gently behind her. She waved to her family, who were clustered together up front. Small tear rivers were running down her face.

Dad's head was high. He was smiling so hard I thought his cheeks would break. His tie flapped over his shoulder, but he didn't seem to notice. Or care.

He looked about college-age. Like photos of him from when I was a baby. I couldn't believe the difference. I just stared and stared at him.

When he and Carol finally stopped, his eyes met mine. I could see them go glassy all of a sudden.

He blinked, and a tear slowly dropped off his eyelash.

That was when I lost it. I sobbed just as Reverend Gunness said "Dearly beloved."

But no one seemed to care. I sure didn't. The reverend kept reciting. I kept on crying. Jeff managed to dig the rings out of his

pocket. Dad and Carol said "I will," loudly and clearly.

And when it was all over, the crowd burst into cheers.

The singers' voices rang out again. People were shaking hands, laughing, rushing toward the happy couple.

Mary Anne ran toward me, arms open.

"He did it!" she cried. "He did it!"

We squeezed each other tightly. Mary Anne was crying so hard, her shoulders were heaving. I realized how much this wedding meant to her. Her own life had changed so wonderfully when her dad found happiness. She wanted the same for me.

And that was more important than my horrible foul-up, a casual beach wedding, and an unwanted dress.

I am so lucky.

My eyes misted over again. Before I buried my face into Mary Anne, I spotted something out of the corner of my eye.

It was Jeff's paisley tie, flying high overhead.

140

Shannon

Stoneybrook, December 17
  I have sat for children who wouldn't talk to me. Who cried the minute I walked into their house. Who threatened to chop my head off. Who couldn't stop hitting each other. Who threw food around the house.
  But I have never sat for kids at a wedding. And after today, I may not ever again . . . .

Shannon

"These seats are too hard."

"Do I have to go to Sunday school?"

"I'm firsty!"

"*Thirsty!* Can you say *th*?"

"Fffff."

"How come they have cushions on the floor?"

"Where's Mommy?"

"My collar is too tight."

"Taylor stepped on my shoe!"

Welcome to the Barrett-DeWitt wedding.

The words were flying all around me. Who was saying what? I'm not sure (except that Ryan DeWitt is the one who hasn't got the *th* sound yet).

Mallory and I had our hands full.

At first we thought it wouldn't be too bad. Buddy and Lindsey are the two biggest mischief makers, and they were to be in the wedding, as ring bearer and flower girl.

So our mission was to stay in the back pew with the remaining children of Mrs. Barrett (Suzi and Marnie) and Franklin (Taylor, Madeleine, and Ryan).

No other kids were there. Mrs. Barrett said that kids often are not invited to weddings.

I thought that was kind of cruel.

Until we sat with the kids in church.

"I have to go I have to go I have to go!" Madeleine said, tugging on my nice new silk blouse.

"I'll take her," Mallory whispered.

An older couple was walking down the aisle. The wife was arm in arm with an usher. She and her husband gave us a withering glance (I read that expression in a book and it's *perfect*).

Fortunately it was still early. The organist was playing softly in the choir loft overhead. Guests were straggling in.

The three ushers were dressed in gray morning coats, which are like tuxes with long tails. One of them looked a little bored, until he saw the kids.

He wandered over to us, smiling, and held out a quarter in his open palm. "See this?" he asked.

The kids nodded. The usher rubbed his hands together and opened them again. They were empty.

"Oops, I see it!" he suddenly exclaimed, then reached behind Taylor's ear and pulled out — the quarter.

"Whoa!" Taylor said in awe.

As the kids oohed and aahed, a woman walked up behind the usher and said, "Hrrrrmph. I'm a friend of the bride."

"Oops, excuse me." The usher took the woman's arm and guided her to a seat.

"I can do that trick," Suzi said. "Shannon, can I have a quarter?"

"Sssh," I urged.

"I have a nickel," Taylor offered.

Suzi frowned. "It might not work with a nickel."

"We're back!" shouted Madeleine. "They have *wooden* toilets — "

"*Madeleine, shhh!*" Mallory hissed, her face turning bright red.

"This is boring," Suzi commented.

"Don't say that," Taylor warned her. "Your mom is getting married."

"Why?" Suzi asked.

Taylor rolled his eyes. "Because she's old. She has to have a husband!"

"Whaaat?" I spoke up. "No *law* says a woman has to have a husband."

"Your mom is marrying Franklin because she loves him," Mallory explained.

"Eeeewwwww." Taylor and Suzi broke into giggles.

"Who do *you* love, Mallory? Ben Hobart?" Suzi teased.

Mal turned beet red.

WHONNNNNNNK!

The organ suddenly blared out. Madeleine

144

screamed. Marnie jumped into Mallory's lap. Ryan burst into hysterical tears.

A loud fanfare began. Now lots of guests were arriving. The ushers were running around like penguins. I heard a voice saying, "She's here!"

I lifted Ryan to my shoulder and stood up. Mallory was already walking Marnie back and forth.

"Look, Marnie," Suzi called out above the music. "It's Barney! Look!" She began grinning, moving stiffly, and clapping her hands. "Hi, boys and girls!"

"Shhhh!" said a man a few rows ahead of us.

Suzi plopped down into the pew. She looked crushed. "I was just trying to cheer her up."

"I thought you were trying to scare her," Taylor remarked.

"*Sssshhhh!*" Mallory and I said.

With a frustrated sigh, Taylor sat next to Suzi, arms folded.

"Too noisy!" Ryan cried out.

"It's *music*," Madeleine explained.

Suzi began sniffling. She was still smarting from the stranger who had shushed her.

"*TOO NOISY!*" Ryan shrieked.

"Time to go," I whispered to Mallory. I

walked toward the center aisle with Ryan. My instructions had been clear: If any of the kids started being a major nuisance during the ceremony, they were to be brought to the church nursery in the basement.

The ceremony hadn't started yet, but I knew it was naptime for Ryan. And one of the first things a baby-sitter learns is that a missed nap makes a cranky toddler.

I zipped out into the aisle. I turned toward the back of the church.

I came face-to-face with Buddy and Lindsey. Behind them was a line of ushers and bridesmaids, arm in arm. Stacey was the second bridesmaid. She was looking at me as if I'd lost my mind.

Gulp. Wrong aisle.

DA-DAHH-DA-DAAAAAHHH! The organist was playing a wedding march. The ceremony had begun.

I spun around. Ryan clutched my shoulders tighter.

"Daddy!" he yelled.

Sure enough, Franklin was at the alter, waiting for Mrs. Barrett. He smiled at Ryan and waved.

"WANNA GO TO DADDY!"

I *flew* into the side aisle. Ryan and I were

out the door and heading for the nursery before he could utter another peep.

How was the wedding?

Beats me. I spent it watching a little boy
asleep in a portable crib.

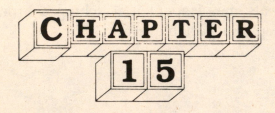

CHAPTER 15

Stacey

Stoneybrook, December 17

A wedding is hard work. Take it from me, the experienced bridesmaid of the BSC! I thought, hey, piece of cake. A stroll down the aisle, lots of teeth, listen to the preacher, cry a little, then book. The bride does all the work.

Boy, was I wrong....

"Oh, you look adorable!" said Andrea the bridesmaid as she touched up my eyeliner.

Jennifer, the other bridesmaid, smiled at my reflection in the mirror of the women's room in the church. "I wish I had skin like that."

"I wish I had her hair," remarked Randi, Mrs. Barrett's sister and maid of honor.

Andrea, Jennifer, and Randi were much older than I was. At first I felt uncomfortable about that. But they were so nice to me.

And it felt *great* to be fussed over.

"Arrrgh!" Randi was frantically trying to keep her hair from coming to a point on the left side of her head. "Great, my sister's a bride, and I'm the Bride of Frankenstein."

"Where are my flowers?" Jennifer asked. "Flowers? Oh, flowers? Where did you go?"

"Here, flowers!" Andrea called out, then whistled as if she were calling a dog.

Randi cracked up. "Aw-roooo! Arf! Arf!"

The door opened up and an old woman walked in. "Hello, girls," she said, looking around the room. "Is there a little pooch in here?"

"No, ma'am, it was the maid of honor," Andrea replied with a straight face.

Jennifer, Randi, and I *howled*.

The woman gave us a curious smile and

gestured toward one of the stalls. "I imagine that must belong to you — or else this is some fancy church."

We looked in to see a corsage propped up behind a toilet paper roll. "*That's* where I put them!" Jennifer said.

I didn't think I'd make it upstairs. My stomach hurt from laughing so much. It was like a BSC meeting, only older.

Somehow we managed to leave the women's room looking dignified. Calm.

We walked upstairs to the front hallway of the church. The organ was honking away. The ushers were busy ushing. Buddy and Lindsey were standing around looking frightened.

"Stacey," Randi said, "can you remind the kids what they have to do?"

I gave Buddy and Lindsey a big, reassuring smile. I descibed everything we had done the night before, in our rehearsal at the church.

The front door was open. As I was talking, I could see a stretch limo pull up to the front.

"She's here!" someone called out.

"She's here! . . . She's here! . . . She's here! . . ." voices repeated all around us. The ushers practically ran the last few guests to their seats. Randi hurried over to me again. "Stacey, can you tell the organist the bride is here?"

I scampered up a spiral staircase to the choir

loft. The organist was playing away, rocking from side to side. I waved to catch his attention. "She's here!" I yelled.

"She's here!" my voice echoed in the church. Ugh. I was mortified.

I raced downstairs. As I passed the open front door, I looked outside.

My breath caught in my throat.

Have you ever tuned into the Oscars early, to see the stars sliding out of their limos, waving to the crowd of gawking people? That's what it was like when Mrs. Barrett emerged from the car in front of the church.

To begin with, Mrs. Barrett is stunning. She has long, silky, chestnut hair and an enormous smile, like a model's. In knock-around clothes, she looks fabulous. In a long, white, beaded, antique wedding gown with a plunging neckline?

Dazzling.

The beads glittered like crazy as Mrs. Barrett stepped out. The material was so fine it looked almost liquid. I could not take my eyes off her.

"Stacey, give me a hand," Randi said.

I followed her outside. As Mrs. Barrett stepped onto the sidewalk, Randi and I lifted the train of her gown off the ground.

We walked behind Mrs. Barrett into the church. She took a few steps into the carpeted outer hallway. Randi and I spread out her train smoothly.

"Thanks," Mrs. Barrett whispered.

"You look gorgeous!" I blurted out.

"You too," she said with a wink.

"Pssst, Stacey! Come on!" Andrea called.

I turned around. The bridesmaids and ushers were lined up, arm in arm. Buddy and Lindsey were already walking up the aisle, and so were Jennifer and her usher-partner. The next usher in line, whose name was Greg, was waiting for me, with his arm outstretched. I linked my arm in his. We gave each other a smile (don't worry, he was my dad's age).

Have you ever been in a formal wedding? You have to walk in time to the music. *Slow* music. It's so unnatural, like slo-mo replay. You think your feet are going to fall asleep between steps.

A baby's voice cried out something, but I was too nervous to pay attention.

Greg and I stepped into the aisle. At that moment, Shannon appeared out of nowhere, smack in front of the procession, holding Ryan DeWitt. When she saw us, she turned the color of Mrs. Barrett's dress.

What was she doing? For a moment I panicked. I thought she wanted to give Ryan to

me. But the next thing I knew, she was heading for the side of the church.

That was the last I saw of her until after the wedding.

Greg was starting to shake. I looked at him and realized he was on the verge of laughing.

We made it to the altar with straight faces, the ushers and Buddy on the right, the bridesmaids and Lindsey on the left. Franklin was already there, waiting. He had this eager, boyish look on his face.

It was kind of funny turning around and seeing a whole church full of people's backs. Everyone was watching for Mrs. Barrett. If I'd done a dance, yawned, or picked my nose, no one would have noticed.

Except maybe the kids in the back row. They were squirming like crazy, looking at everything, whispering and laughing. Poor Mallory.

You should have heard the church when Mrs. Barrett entered. The gasps were louder than the organ music. I glanced at Franklin and he looked as if he were going to cry.

Somehow, when *she* walked down the aisle, her slow steps looked graceful and natural. She turned her head slowly from side to side, nodding slightly. Her smile was so warm and unforced. *How could she not be petrified?* I didn't understand it.

154

Do you know when Mrs. Barrett lost her poise? When she saw Franklin. She swallowed. I could hear a breath hitch in her throat. Her eyes welled up.

But the smile never left her face. For two divorced parents who'd been fighting for the last few weeks, they looked *soooo* in love.

The minister began the service. A cry of "Mommy!" rang out from the back of the church. Mrs. Barrett and Franklin burst out laughing.

That loosened things up. All the guests laughed, too. Mrs. Barrett turned and waved to the kids.

Next thing we knew, little Marnie Barrett had toddled up to the altar, pacifier hanging from her mouth. Mallory was behind her, looking horrified.

Mrs. Barrett did a double-take. "Oh!" she exclaimed.

Marnie beamed. She threw her arms around her mom's legs and hugged her tightly.

"Awwwwww . . ." said the congregation.

Mrs. Barrett gently put her hand out to Mallory, as if to say, "It's all right."

The minister looked at Mrs. Barrett. She smiled and shrugged.

"You know," the minister announced with a chuckle, "people always say, 'Never take kids to a wedding; they steal all the attention.' "

Everyone laughed politely.

"Well, I disagree," he went on. "For these two people before you are not only giving each other their love, but their families as well. I can think of no deeper, more personal Christmas gift than that — and I'm happy that their children are all close by on this day. . . ."

What a cool minister.

You know what? Marnie stayed throughout the entire ceremony. She didn't move a muscle.

That, I think, was my favorite part of the wedding.

Claudia

Palo City, December 17

What a trip. I not only got to see a grate weding, but also got valubile on the job traning. Plus I lerned some brand new skcills. PLUS PLUS I got pade for it (well, sort of).

The ~~recep recepesh~~ party after the weding was so much fun! It was in Mr. Shafer's back yard, with an enormis yellow and white tent and a long buffay table.

Stuert ~~the~~ caterer did not come to the party. Neither did Lyel the flowerist. It's too bad, because everything looked wonderful. Exept the grape leves did not taist AT ALL like graps! Yuck. I had to wash down the flaver with a big bole of chocklit mouse.

I regret only one thing. I will not be hear when the pixtures come back....

"Have you tried the grape leaves? They're exquisite," said a man with slicked-back short hair and sunglasses to a woman with slicked-back short hair and sunglasses.

Click.

A green-eyed woman was tracing in the air with a celery stick and telling a friend, "So if you add the incremental cost of insurance weighed against the rutabagas and kumquats and cabbage and horsetails . . ." (Well, not those exact words, but my attention was drifting.)

Click.

During a break in the music, a band member let Jeff play the drums.

Click.

Mrs. Bruen, who was slicing the duck, held up a drumstick and smiled. Next to her, the vegetarian We ♥ Kids Club all shook their fingers at her.

Click. Click. Click.

In case you didn't know, that was me clicking. I was walking around the Schafer backyard (oops, the Schafer/Olson backyard) with the coolest camera.

Mr. Schafer had given it to me for the day, with several rolls of film. He and Carol had hired a professional photographer, but he also wanted some candids. Dawn had insisted that *I* should be the one to do the candids.

And that was how I added another job to my California résumé: Florist, Catering Consultant, Hair Stylist, and Photographer.

Anyway, the camera was a 35-millimeter SLR autofocus with auto-advance. In English, that means you look through the viewfinder and shoot. Mr. Schafer calls it a Ph.D. camera (which he says stands for "Press Here, Dummy").

Maybe so. But a good artist knows how to take advantage of new technologies. And I've had plenty of experience with cameras. So I took rapid-fire shots by keeping my finger pressed on the button. I took a picture of Dawn, Mary Anne, Kristy, Claudia, Sunny, Maggie, Jill, *and me*, by using the self-timer. I tried a double exposure, to make it look as if

Jeff were having a conversation with himself. I shot from all different angles: from the ground, from the point of view of the roast duck, from the top of a ladder.

After some of Mr. Schafer's friends gave him a toast, they lifted him onto their shoulders. *Click.* Dawn's grandparents and Carol's mom, who had arrived the night before and stayed at a hotel, gave their own tearful toasts. *Click. Click.* Carol got in front of the band and sang a song called, "What Are You Doing the Rest of Your Life?" to her new husband. *Click X 7.*

Did this seem like work? No way!

Finally, Dawn got up and took the microphone from the bandstand.

"Um, I just wanted to say that I have the best dad in the world. . . ." she began.

"Hear hear!" someone shouted, over loud applause.

"At first it was, well, *hard* to see him falling in love with Carol. I guess it was hard for Carol to know it was hard for me, too. Does that make sense?" Everyone chuckled, then Dawn went on: "But she and Dad stuck by each other, and both of them stuck by me."

"Always, sweetheart." In the silence, Carol's soft voice carried throughout the tent.

Dawn took a deep breath. "What I'm trying to say is I always knew how lucky Carol was.

But now I know how lucky Dad is, too. And I'll be so sad to go back to Connecticut." Her voice caught. Quickly she held up her glass of champagne (well, it just had a teeny bit at the bottom). "So here's a toast to Dad . . . and my new mom!"

"*Yeah!* Go, Dawn! Wooo-hooo!" Kristy shouted. Luckily, other people were cheering, too.

It was the nicest toast of the party.

I took a million more photos. Then I spotted Kristy at the buffet table. My poor, neglected little stomach gave a gurgle. I joined her.

As we were stuffing our faces, Mrs. Bruen appeared at the rear screen door. "Would you two come in here a minute?"

Uh-oh. Had we dropped Milk Duds on the Persian rug? Left the hairspray too near the whipped cream?

She led us to the living room. It looked like a warehouse. Wedding presents were stacked higher than my head — on the sofa, on the coffee table, in front of the wall unit.

I almost didn't notice the huge Christmas tree leaning against the corner wall, wrapped up with string.

Mrs. Bruen pointed to an old cardboard box next to the tree. "I brought the decorations down from the attic. Now, I have to go back out and help with the party. You think you two girls can set up the tree before Jack and Carol open their wedding presents?"

Mrs. Bruen was smiling like a kid.

"Give us ten minutes!" Kristy exclaimed.

I put my camera down. We had work to do.

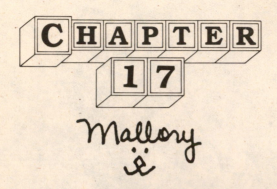

CHAPTER 17

Mallory

Stoneybrook, December 17

Halfway through the wedding service,
I thought about changing my name.
To Ebenezer. Ebenezer S. Pike. Keeping
four kids quiet through a wedding is
not hard — it's impossible! When Marnie
got away from me and ran to her mom,
I thought I'd die.

Well, that worked out. Fortunately.
(Although I don't know if Mrs. Barrett
will ever hire me again.) Marnie was
adorable, and the kids behaved pretty
well. And I really liked the minister.
He made me think about family and
relationships, and Christmas, and a
certain former boyfriend . . . .

164

Marnie was a star. No question.

She really milked it. After the vows, I tried to convince her to come back to me. I grinned from the side of the pews. I waved. I held up a milk bottle. Marnie just kept shaking her head.

I looked like a fool.

The ceremony ended. Down the aisle marched Mrs. Barrett, holding Franklin's hand — and Marnie's.

I ran to the back of the church. The kids were drawing pictures in the hymnals (I don't know who had brought the crayons).

I quickly returned the books to their holders.

"Hey, I was drawing a dragon!" Taylor protested.

"This is a church book," I reminded him.

"I know. It was St. George's dragon," he said, as if that made it all right.

"It's time to stand in the receiving line," I said.

"What's that?" Madeleine asked.

"Your mom and dad, the wedding party, and you guys all have to line up in the front hall. You greet all the wedding guests."

"Boring," Suzi murmured.

"Just think," I said, "this is the first thing you'll be doing together as a family."

Taylor beamed at Suzi. "Hey! You're my *sister*!"

"Mine too!" Madeleine added.

They jumped up and down, hugging each other. Then we wound our way out to the receiving line.

Mrs. Barrett and Franklin were deep in conversation with some of the guests. Next to them, Marnie was holding court.

"How old are you, dear?" a balding, round-faced man asked.

Marnie held up five fingers. "Two."

We took our places. Mrs. Barrett and Franklin showered the kids with hugs and kisses. Afterward the kids stood shyly, answered some of the questions, and kept the goofing off to a minimum.

When Shannon came upstairs with Ryan, she looked fresh and relaxed. "How was the ceremony?" she asked. "Oh, I am *soooo* jealous."

All I could do was laugh.

After leaving the receiving line, the guests waited outside the church. They tossed bird seed as Mrs. Barrett and Franklin ran to their limo. (Yes, bird seed. The church wouldn't allow rice.)

I still can't figure that one out.

Anyway, Buddy, Suzi, Marnie, Taylor, Lindsey, Madeleine, and Ryan all piled into the limo, too. I did not have to go with them. I was free. Mrs. Barrett said the kids would have plenty of relatives and older kids to watch over them at the reception.

What a relief. Now I could go home — to a house full of kids.

Oh, well. At least I had a bedroom there.

But Shannon and I stayed at the church a little longer. A Peterson truck had pulled in front of the church. Peterson's is a nursery in Stoneybrook.) Two workers began unloading all kinds of Christmasy stuff — plants, flowers, pine boughs, and a Christmas tree.

We watched them take it into the church. I caught a whiff of pine.

"Mmmmmm," I said.

"That is my favorite smell in the world," Shannon replied. "Can you believe Christmas is eight days away?"

Eight days?

I'd been so wrapped up in the wedding, I hadn't been keeping count.

But it wasn't only the wedding. Something else had spoiled the holiday for me.

My fight with Ben. After that, I'd kind of gotten out of the spirit.

I didn't have much time to get back into it, did I?

I quickly said good-bye and walked home.

Mom, Margo, and Claire were there. Everyone else had gone to a movie. I was exhausted. I went straight to my room and flopped on the bed.

But I couldn't nap. I was still thinking about Ben. And the caroling, which should have been happening right about that time. Boy, had I messed that one up.

I wanted to call Ben. But what could I say? He was furious at me, and he had every right to be.

The minister had talked about the season of giving and receiving. Some giver I was. I'd let all those kids get excited about singing, then taken the excitement away from them.

Ebenezer Pike. It did fit.

I imagined what the caroling would have been like. I pictured Ben and me, standing together. He would be singing away at the top of his lungs. I'd be croaking along, way out of tune. The kids would be mouthing, whispering, shouting. But none of that mattered. In my mind it sounded great.

Now what? Could we let the whole season go by without talking to each other? Not even saying "Merry Christmas"?

I sat up.

I went into my parents' room and tapped out his number on their phone.

"Hello?" It was Mr. Hobart.

"Hi, it's Mallory. Is Ben there?"

"Well, Merry Christmas to you, Mal. As a matter of fact, he's right here."

Roit heah.

I *love* that accent.

But Ben didn't come on right away. I heard Mr. Hobart say, in a muffled voice, "*Talk* to her."

Then, "Yeah?"

"Hi, Ben. It's me."

"Hi."

"Um . . . I called to say I'm sorry."

"You are?"

"I did a stupid thing. I should have thought about our plans before I said yes to Mrs. Barrett."

"Oh. You're not still mad?"

"Me?"

"You sounded mad the last time we talked."

"So did you."

"I was." He quickly added, "I shouldn't

have been. You messed up, but it wasn't that big a deal. We didn't have to, like, break up over it."

"I know."

"We could have gone caroling another day."

"We still can, really. I mean, there are still eight more days till Christmas."

"Want to go?" Ben asked.

I laughed. "Okay!"

"Yeah?"

"Yeah!"

Now Ben was laughing. "That was easy! Why didn't we think of that before?"

"I don't know. I guess we were too angry."

Ben sighed. "Dumb, huh?"

"Real dumb."

"Well, what day should we sing?"

We decided the next day, Sunday, would be best. As soon as we hung up, we called the parents of the kids who were supposed to go caroling in the first place. Everyone said yes except the Marshalls (they were going out to dinner).

Guess who else wanted to go? Adam, Jordan, Byron, Nicky, Vanessa, Margo, and Claire Pike, that's who.

We had a chorus of seventeen on Sunday.

We met at our house first for a rehearsal — which was more like a party. Dad and Mom served us hot chocolate and cookies.

We hit the streets at seven o'clock.

"Okay, we'll sing 'Jingle Bells' first," I announced. I figured we'd go to the Clements' house. They're this nice couple who have a son in college.

Their son opened the door. He had beard stubble, a scowl, and must have been six foot four.

"Jing."

Only one syllable was sung, from only one voice. Mine. Everyone else just froze.

Then the guy broke into a smile. "Hey-y-y-y! Christmas carolers! Mom! Dad!"

Well, we started again, and all three Clementses joined in.

Next, this older couple, the Goldmans, invited us in for cake and cookies and fruitcake. When we left, only the fruitcake remained.

Adam started feeling nauseous right afterward. He pulled through, but he ate none of the cookies the Braddocks offered us.

We sang for Mary Anne's and Dawn's parents. We sang for the Kishis. And the Prezziosos and the Arnolds.

171

The kids' cheeks got rosier and rosier. Their voices got louder and louder. And their lyrics got weirder and weirder.

When James Hobart sang "Deck the halls with bowling balls," all of them wanted to outdo him.

Mathew came up with "Jingle Bells, liver smells, throw it all away . . ."

Jake's contribution was "Joy to the world, my hair is curled . . ."

Becca sang out, "Rudolph the Red-Nosed Reindeer, wasn't wearing any clothes . . ." (That was the least funny one, but it got the most giggles.)

Not to be outdone, Jamie Newton came up with "O Christmas tree, O Christmas tree, don't fall on my head." (Well, he's four.)

But the nicest part of the whole evening came at the end. We stopped at the corner near my house and just sang for each other.

"Silent night, holy night,
All is calm, all is bright. . . .

Above us, stars glittered and faded in the clear sky. Colored lights blazed in the houses around us. And in just about every window was a curious face, listening silently.

Ben and I put our arms around each other.

I wasn't worrying about Christmas spirit anymore.

CHAPTER 18

Jeff

Palo City, December 17
    Dad and Carol had a
party. With a real tent.
And a band. Most of
the food stunk, though.
Who ever heard of
eating duck? That is
disgusting. Plus these
cold, slimy leaves rolled
around rice balls. Gag
me with a shovel.
    The carrot wedding
cake was good.
    Dawn gave a ~~real dumb~~ very, nice
toast. Then Carol cut the
176

cake and shoved a piece in Dad's mouth. He got some icing on his nose. That was funny!

But the best part came after. In the living room....

Mrs. Bruen made me change that part about Dawn's toast. She said it was okay to make fun of food but not of people. She was really bossy the whole day long.

And it *was* a dumb toast.

You know what else? There were NO KIDS at that party. I mean, some little kids were there — like, six and four and eight years old. Also some teenagers. But nobody the right age.

Grown-ups can be so boring. They kept asking me the same questions, about a thousand times. I felt like wearing a sign around my neck that said:

JEFF.

JACK'S SON.

TEN YEARS OLD.

FIFTH GRADE.

OF COURSE I'VE GROWN — I'M A KID.

I mean, what am I supposed to say to them? "And how old are *you*?" or "Well, you sure *haven't* grown."

I smiled a lot.

Anyway, Mrs. Bruen was in charge of the party. She snuck me an extra piece of cake, so I wasn't mad at her for being bossy.

While I stuffed it in my mouth, she ate a piece, too. On a plate with a fork.

She grinned at me. A little hunk of icing was stuck to her lip.

I was going to miss Mrs. Bruen. She didn't look too unhappy, though.

"Did you find another job?" I asked.

She laughed. "Trying to get rid of me?"

"No! But I mean, after today, with Carol moving in . . ."

"One person joining the household, one leaving. Sounds to me as if there won't be any less work for me, does it?"

"You mean they're not going to fire you?"

Mrs. Bruen looked shocked. "Goodness, no! Just between you and me, Carol makes your dad look neat. They want to double my hours!"

Yeeee-haaah! I was so happy. I wanted to jump up and down. "Good," I said.

Mrs. Bruen gave me a sly smile. "Worried, weren't you?"

"Me? Naaah."

I was cool. She didn't suspect a thing.

When the party was over and all the guests had left, Dad said he wanted to open presents.

"Aren't you tired, Jack?" Carol asked.

"Never too tired for *that*," he answered.

That's just what I would have said.

Dad, Carol, Mrs. Bruen, Dawn, Kristy, Claudia, Mary Anne, and I all went inside. And guess what? Someone had put a Christmas tree in the living room! With lights and decorations and everything.

"Wow! Where did that come from?" I asked.

"Santa Claus," Kristy said.

"Yeah, right."

"It's lovely," Carol said.

Everybody oohed and aahed.

Dad sat on the couch. "Ohhhhhh, my feet," he said.

He put them up on a box on the coffee table.

"Careful!" Carol said. "It's fragile!"

"So are my feet," Dad replied. But he took them down anyway.

Carol opened the fragile box. Inside it was a set of shrunken coffee cups. At least that's how they looked to me.

"Ooh, demitasse," Carol said. "How beautiful."

I guess. Like, for a doll house.

Next, Dad opened a box and took out a bowl. Then Carol opened another box. It had a bowl, too. They opened four more boxes, and two of *them* had bowls.

"You could go bowling," Claudia said. (She's funny sometimes.)

Mrs. Bruen started picking up the empty boxes. "Sit. Relax," Dad told her. "The party's over."

"I have to move them," she said. "The movers won't have any place to put Carol's furniture."

Yuck. I had forgotten about that.

Mary Anne was staring at this tall, narrow box. It said FRAGILE on the side, too. "What could this be?" she asked.

Carol opened it. She pulled out a shiny statue. It was a clown in a black-and-white polka dot costume. He looked like he was crying. A long electrical cord stuck out the back.

"I think it's a lamp," Claudia said.

Carol plugged it into the wall. She found two buttons on the side and pressed one.

The clown lit up from the inside. And his frown curved upward into a smile.

Then Carol pressed the other button, and the clown began singing an opera song.

Dad looked as if the clown were made of

buggers. "Turn that thing off!" he said.

Kristy quickly pressed the button.

Nobody said anything for a few seconds. Then Carol started laughing. "I'm sorry. . . . Sorry. Let's open another one."

"What? What do you think of it?" Dad asked with a funny smile.

Carol tried not to laugh, but it didn't work. *That is the ugliest gift I have ever seen!*

Everyone started laughing. Kristy was rolling on the floor. Claudia and Dawn looked as if they were holding each other up. Mary Anne's eyes were watering. Even Mrs. Bruen was laughing.

Dad's shoulders were bouncing up and down. Then he calmed down and patted the clown on the head. "Maybe we should keep him."

"Aaaaugh!" Dawn screamed. "I will never *ever* visit you again if you do." She pulled the plug out. Then she ran to Mrs. Bruen's pile of throw-out boxes and tried to stuff the clown in.

"Go! Go! Go! Go!" Kristy called out.

Everybody joined in. Except me.

I thought the gift was kind of cool.

Dad and Carol kept opening. Most of the other stuff was, like, kitchen things. And a few more bowls. Zzzzzz.

When they were down to the last few boxes, the phone rang. Dad went into the kitchen to get it.

I could hear him yelling. Everyone got nervous.

A long time later, he came back.

"It's gone," he announced. "All of it."

"*Whaaaat?*" Carol said.

"The furniture?" Dawn ventured.

Dad nodded. "The van was stolen. They found it in a lot just off the freeway, halfway to San Diego. It was stripped and completely empty."

No one said a word. I looked at Mrs. Bruen. She looked at Carol.

Carol was totally still. Then she started laughing again.

"I — I'm not joking, sweetheart," Dad said.

"I know," Carol answered. "But . . . but it's okay."

"It is?" Dad asked.

"I never liked that furniture in the first place!"

"Really?" I asked.

Dad put his hands on his hips. "Wait a minute. You were dead set on bringing that stuff here. You said you . . . you *came of age* with the wall unit."

"I know, but that's just because you were

trying to make decisions for me," Carol said. "It was the *principle*, Jack. But let's face it, this house has enough furniture, and it's so much nicer than mine was."

I imagined the lava lamp in the robber's house. I hope he enjoyed it.

Dad smiled. He sat down next to Carol. They smooched.

"Ew," I said. I couldn't look.

Everyone else said, "Awwww."

Grown-ups. Weird. What did I tell you?

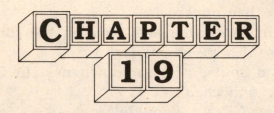

CHAPTER 19

Kristy

Palo City, December 18
    Today was Dawn's big surprise farewell party!
    Some surprise.
    I could have killed Sunny at that wedding reception when she said, "See you at the party"....

Yes, she did say that. As she and the other guests were leaving, right before Mr. Schafer and Carol began opening their presents.

"What party?" Dawn asked.

"I — I meant at the airport!" Sunny stammered.

"But aren't we all having brunch before then?" Dawn said.

"That's what she meant," Maggie stuttered.

"Oh."

" 'Bye!" I have never seen the members of the We ♥ Kids Club move so fast.

Very skillful, huh?

Oh, well. Dawn didn't seem to get it. Or else she hid it really well.

This was our alibi: We were going to meet at Sunny's, then go out to a health-food restaurant for brunch. (As if I would ever agree to do that.)

The night after the wedding, Dawn, Claudia, Mary Anne, and I stayed up late chatting. Mary Anne, of course, had packed her suitcase already (don't ask me when she did it).

The rest of us had to pack in the morning. For me, that was no big deal. But Claudia — well, Claudia can make a production out of packing a lunchbag.

Have you ever seen a rabbit in the jaws of

a snake? You know, like on an educational TV show? Gross, I know, but that was what Claudia's suitcase looked like. You could not imagine it ever closing.

"How did I get all this stuff here?" she muttered.

"You didn't," I replied. "You went shopping at the mall."

"I know, but it was only a couple of T-shirts for me and some books and shorts for Janine," Claudia said. "Oh, and the California Angels windbreaker for Dad, and Mom's hat."

"And the sunglasses and a couple of Nancy Drews," Mary Anne added.

"Which you could have bought back home," I added.

Claudia gave me a puppyish look. "Kristy, do you have any room in your duffel bag?"

Guess who had to drag home a two-ton duffel bag later that day?

Anyway, we got off to a late start. That made me nervous. "Brunch" was supposed to be at ten-thirty. That meant we only had a couple of hours to party. Then we'd have to run back and get ready to go. The drive to John Wayne Airport was about half an hour (allowing for traffic), and our flight was scheduled for two-thirty P.M.

Cutting it close, I know. But I hadn't figured

in the Kishi Factor, so we were even worse off. We got to Sunny's at 11:03.

We let Dawn ring the bell.

Rumble, rumble. Shhhhh. Giggle, giggle.

Unbelievable. It sounded like an army of mice had taken over the house. I *know* Dawn heard that.

Then Sunny opened the door. She had this huge, unnatural smile. "Hiiiiiiii! Come on in. We're just about ready to leave for brunch."

Dawn took one step into the house, and then —

"*SURPRIIIIIISE!*"

Flash! went a camera.

Dawn gasped. The living room was full. Jill and Maggie were there, and Mr. and Mrs. Winslow, some kids from Dawn's school, and a few of the W♥KC's favorite charges.

I didn't know Dawn's school friends, but I recognized the little kids — Daffodil and Clover Austin (who are eight and five); the DeWitt boys, eight-year-old Erick and six-year-old Ryan (yes, another Ryan DeWitt, and no, not related); and Stephie Robertson, who's eight.

Draped across the room was a huge piece of paper that said BON VOYAGE, DAWN! It was signed with a personal message from everyone.

"Did you know we were here?" Daffodil called out.

"No!" Dawn replied. "Oh, I can't believe this! You *guys*!"

She hugged everybody, squealing and saying "I'll miss you!" each time.

Mr. Winslow kept moving around, taking pictures of Dawn's reaction.

"There's a cake!" Erick called out. "Sunny won't let *us* eat it till *you* have the first piece."

A cake? Even I didn't know about that.

Dawn went straight to the dining room. There, Whitney Cater was carefully unwrapping paper plates and setting them on a table full of food (most of which looked completely inedible). Whitney's twelve and she has Down's Syndrome. Dawn was once hired to sit for her, but Whitney thought Dawn just wanted to be friends. She was hurt when she found out the truth, but she and Dawn talked it out and became very close. Whitney's an honorary W♥KC member now.

"Hi!" Whitney called out.

"Oh, Whitney . . ." Dawn and Whitney threw their arms around each other.

Whitney began crying. "I'm going to miss you so much."

"Me too."

It came out more like "Me too-hoo-hoo."

(Yes, Dawn was crying, too-hoo-hoo.)

I was sad, but I couldn't cry. I mean, I *was* going to see Dawn in Stoneybrook the next week.

Mary Anne? Well, she wasn't doing so well in the dry-eye department, but what else is new?

"Hey, Dawn, did you have any cake yet?" Erick the Persistent called out.

Dawn let go of Whitney and finally looked at the cake.

It wasn't a cake, really. It was a work of art. It had been made to look like Dawn's face — blonde hair, sunglasses, freckles, and a big smile, all made of frosting.

"Oh . . ." Dawn said.

"Awesome," Claudia added. "Who made it?"

"Me and Joanna and my daddy," answered a teeny voice.

Off to the side, practically hidden by all the people, was Stephie Robertson. She's usually so bubbly, but that day she looked glum.

"Stephie, it's *breathtaking*! I don't even want to eat it, it's so beautiful."

"Oh, *no*," Erick moaned.

Mr. Winslow handed her a Polaroid photo of the cake. "For your memory book," he said.

Dawn was shaking her head in disbelief.

"Well, I guess I should cut it, huh?"

"Yeeeeaaaahhhh!" screamed most of the kids.

"I'll do it," volunteered Whitney.

She began slicing pieces. Mary Anne and Sunny helped her put them on plates.

"Mmmmmm," Dawn said as she ate the first piece. "I love banana cake, Stephie."

Stephie nodded.

"Stephie, are you okay?"

She folded her arms and looked off to the side. Her eyes were red. "I'm mad at you."

"Because I'm leaving?"

"Yeah." Stephie choked back a sniffle.

Poor kid. She adores Dawn. Not too long ago, Stephie was this shy, asthmatic girl who hardly ever went outside. Then she and Dawn really hit it off. Slowly Stephie came out of her shell. Even her asthma improved.

"I'll be back to visit, I promise," Dawn said. "And I'll write you tons of letters. Will you write me?"

"I already did." She pulled a folded-up piece of looseleaf paper out of her pocket.

"May I read it?"

"Uh-huh."

I couldn't tell what the letter said, but it made Dawn cry again. Later she showed it to me:

BON VOYAGE, DAWN!

Kristy

DEAR DAWN,
   WHY DO YOU HAVE TO LIVE IN
CONETICUT? YOU CAN LIVE HEAR ITS
MUCH BETTER. I ONCE SAW A
BIG TRUCK PULLING A HOLE HOUSE
DOWN THE STREET. AIRPLANES
ARE BIGGER THAN TRUCKS. SO YOU
CAN FLY YOUR HOUSE HEAR. THEN
YOUL'L BE HOME WHEN YOUR IN
CALIFORNIA.
   I ASKED DADDY IF WE COUD DO
THAT TO OUR HOUS AND HE SAID NO.
   IF YOU CANT DO THAT EITHER,
MAYBE YOU CAN TAKE ME WITH
YOU.
   I LOVE YOU, DAWN. ALWAYS
AND FOREVER. EVEN IF YOU
HAVE TO LIVE FAR AWAY.
                    STEPHIE

Dawn had a great time at the party. But she
said nothing beat that letter.

CHAPTER 20

LOGAN

STONEYBROOK, DECEMBER 20

YES, FOLKS, IT WAS MOVING DAY FOR
THE BARRETTS AND DEWITTS! AND GUESS
WHICH BSC MEMBER THEY CHOSE TO
HELP THEM DO THE DIRTY WORK?

YOURS TRULY.

I WAS KIND OF LOOKING FORWARD
TO IT. I FIGURED IT WOULD BE A
GOOD WORKOUT, WITHOUT HAVING TO
HIT THE MACHINES IN THE GYM.

I WAS RIGHT ABOUT THE WORKOUT.

BUT I WISH I'D KNOWN FRANKLIN
HAD A PIANO . . . .

"Over — here — okay — Got it? Set it down — Easy — *Auuugh!*"

PLANNNNNK!

Franklin's piano thundered to the floor. It was either that or destroy our backs.

Have you ever tried to lift an upright piano?

If you have, I feel sorry for you. If you haven't, don't.

Franklin does not play the piano. Neither do his kids, although Ryan likes to walk on the keys if someone is holding his hand. The Barretts do not have a piano, nor do any of them want to.

So why were we going through all this?

Because Franklin had the piano in his old house. The previous owner had left it there. Why? He didn't want the hassle of moving it.

Did Franklin follow that man's example? Noooo. He thought the piano would be "a good investment in the future."

Some people have to learn their own lessons.

Anyway, my arms were falling off. I could swear they'd stretched. From now on I'd need a longer shirt sleeve size. "Is this the right place?" I asked.

Still panting for breath, Franklin stepped back and looked around the living room. We had put the piano near a side wall.

"I think so," he said. Then he called out, "Natalie?"

Mrs. Barrett (or I guess she was Mrs. DeWitt now) appeared in the living room archway. She was wearing dusty, paint-stained sweats and her hair was pulled up in a bun. "Franklin, I said the *east* wall!"

Franklin fell to the floor on his back, as if he'd been knocked out. "Newlywed middle-aged man dies in domestic piano-moving incident. Details at eleven."

Mrs. DeWitt laughed. "I guess that means we leave it there."

"Thank you!" Franklin said, springing to his feet. "You see how she and I think alike, Logan? I *knew* we were meant for each other."

He threw his arms around her and started necking.

"Aaaaah! You're filthy!" she screamed.

I turned away. This was embarrassing.

"Look! Pannano!"

Ryan came toddling into the room, followed by Madeleine and Suzi. Guess where they all went?

BANG! CLONK! FOOMP! PLINK!

Mozart it wasn't.

"I'll go unload some of the boxes," Franklin volunteered.

"Logan, would you give the boys a hand in the basement?" Mrs. DeWitt asked. "Their bookcase needs assembling, and then I think the girls need some help upstairs, too."

We both left the recital. Unfortunately there was no escaping the noise, but you got used to it after awhile.

Buddy and Taylor's bedroom was in the basement (it's a small house, and that was the room they picked). Mrs. DeWitt walked downstairs with me. We entered a room that had a bunkbed, boxes, and a bookcase with no shelves (the movers had taken it apart). Buddy and Taylor were rooting around in several boxes, throwing the books all over the floor.

"Now you two *help* Logan, okay?" Mrs. DeWitt asked.

"Okay," they mumbled.

Mrs. DeWitt left.

Taylor yelled out, "*Freckle Juice*! I love that book."

"It's mine!" Buddy protested.

"How do you know?"

"See the box? It says BARRETT, B-A-R-R — "

"I can read."

"Uh, guys?" I said. "You're supposed to help, remember?" I pointed to a stack of shelves the movers had taped together. "Why don't you untape those?"

Well, that took them all of two minutes. As I installed the shelves, they went back to their literary discussion group.

Buddy: "My *Wizard of Oz* has much better pictures than yours."

Taylor: "Oh, yeah? Do you have *Animalia*?"

Buddy: "I did when I was a baby."

Taylor: "I'm not a baby!"

"Yo, fellas!" I cut in. "Why don't you start putting the books on the shelves, okay? Like, in alphabetical order or something."

"I'm not going to let my books touch his," Taylor announced.

"Good. Then mine won't get cooties," Buddy replied.

"Okay, let's split the shelves in half," I suggested.

Taylor's eyes lit up. "Yeah! Like, with karate chops!"

"That's not what he means, dodo," Buddy said.

I don't need to give you the rest of the blow-by-blow. Somehow I managed to negotiate a temporary truce.

Next I went to Lindsey's and Suzi's bedroom, where my assignment was to help Franklin obey all their commands. We moved

the bunkbed to the opposite side of their bedroom. Then we separated the two beds. Then
we put them back together where they had
been in the first place. Then Suzi decided she
wanted to room with Madeleine. Lindsey
stormed off in anger.

I left that one to Franklin.

I fed Marnie and Ryan. I played Chutes and
Ladders with Madeleine. I came to the rescue
when Buddy turned on the washing machine
by mistake and scared the living daylights out
of Taylor.

By the time I had to go, I felt as exhausted
as if I'd had football practice.

But as I was putting on my coat, I saw Suzi
crying in the kitchen, all alone.

I sat next to her. "What's up?" I asked.

"He's . . ." *Sniff.* "He's . . ." *Sniff.* ". . . not
going to find us. I *know* it."

"Who's not going to find you?"

"*Santa.* He's going to go to our old house."

"I'm sure he knows, Suzi."

"No, he doesn't! I wrote him a letter, but
he didn't read it yet."

"How do you know?" I asked.

"*Because,*" Suzi said impatiently, "I told him
to please write back, and he didn't. And besides, he gets millions of letters. Everyone
knows that." She burst into tears. "The new

people are going to get all my toys!"

"Well, uh, then you'll get the toys that the kids who lived here would get, right?"

"What kids?" Suzi snapped. "It was all old people. I'm going to get, like, fat dresses and . . . and sweaters!"

Great suggestion, Logan. Figure this one out.

"Wow, that is a problem," I said. "Hmmmm. The trick is, how do we let Santa know to move the gifts from one house to the next?"

"Mom says we can't use an airplane with a sign."

"What about sending a fax?"

"Silly. Santa doesn't have a fax machine. He's old-fashioned."

"Well, how about leaving him some kind of sign at the old house?"

Suzi thought a minute. Slowly a smile spread across her face. "I know!"

I listened carefully as Suzi told me an idea that was ridiculous and childish.

But brilliant.

CHAPTER 21

Dawn

In a plane somewhere over the Midwest, December 25

I'm finally flying home to Stoneybrook. Eight days after the wedding, a week after my going-away party, three days after my last day of school.

Here we are, looking down on cornfields. Well, I am. Jeff's asleep. Right now Dad and Carol are probably landing in Puerto Vallarta, Mexico, to begin their honeymoon. We drove to the airport together and had the noisiest, most tearful and frantic good-bye of all time. Jeff and I rushed to our gate, they to theirs. It was like a movie!

Boy, am I familiar with this flight. Everything looks the same — the plane, the food (ick), even the view out the window.

But so much has changed since I flew out to Palo City to begin my trip. I was so nervous and confused back then. I felt like I didn't really fit anywhere. Wherever I was, I felt half empty.

I feel different now. I mean, nothing much has changed (well, except Dad's wedding, which is a big deal), but now I feel like I have two wonderful homes. . . .

Dawn

"Rrraumph," said Jeff as he turned in his seat.

I don't know how he could sleep. I could barely sit still, I was so excited about flying back to Connecticut.

I tried to watch the in-flight movie, but I lost the plot line during the opening credits.

Besides, I had my own movie rolling in my head. I kept thinking of the incredible week I'd just had.

Kristy was so sure I knew about my surprise party in advance. She kept insisting I *must* have known. I kept telling her no, I *was* surprised, but she kept saying I couldn't have been. I began feeling like a total doofus for *not* knowing about it.

Finally I hinted I did know. Just to keep her quiet.

But the truth was, I was shocked. And moved.

I had the best time. And I even loved every morsel of that cake, despite the fact that it was made with *way* too much refined sugar.

Actually, I was eating a piece of it when Kristy sounded the alarm.

Phweeeeet! Kristy is the only person I know who would take a referee's whistle to a farewell party.

"Excuse me, but all us Connecticut people have to leave right now!" she called out.

I stuffed the cake into my mouth and looked at my watch. Ten to one.

Yikes! We had overstayed by twenty minutes.

You should have seen Kristy. She got us out of there in about three minutes — and complained that we were too slow.

I'm glad she didn't have a whip with her.

We were lucky. Carol and Dad had loaded the suitcases into the trunk. They were already backing out of the driveway, intending to pick us up.

Dad was a much better driver than he had been on the day of the wedding. He zipped in and out of traffic like a pro, and we got to the airport at 1:20.

That meant we were *early*, so we had plenty of time to cry and hug and cry and gossip and cry and eat and cry.

Jeff kept saying, "You're going to be seeing them in a *week*, Dawn."

Brothers just don't understand.

We stayed to watch the plane leave. I felt sad but excited. Jeff's and my tickets were for December 25, which meant we would get to spend Christmas on both coasts.

I could barely sleep Sunday night. In all the

excitement, I hadn't been able to study very much. And my big exams were coming up on Monday, Tuesday, and Wednesday.

At 2:00 A.M., I started crying in my bed.

The door slowly opened. "Dawn?" said Carol's voice.

I was a little jolted. It was hard to get used to the fact that Carol actually *lived* with us now.

"Hi," I said with a sniffle.

She flicked on the light. "Are you okay?"

I told her what I was worrying about. She listened patiently, then said, "Look. I'm on vacation from work this week. I don't have too much to do. Just a few things to buy for the honeymoon. I'd be happy to be your tutor for the week. I did great in eighth grade, you know."

"Sure," I said. "Thanks."

No question. Dad had made the right choice. I went back to sleep.

Carol was a pretty decent teacher. I got an A− in math, a B in English, a B+ in social studies, and a flat-out A in science.

Wa-hoo! What a relief!

My teachers had been told that I needed my grades before my flight on Christmas. (Lord knows what would have happened if I'd flunked. I guess I'd have had to stay in California and Dad would have been stuck with the ticket.)

I had the sweetest, most wonderful Christmas Eve ever. First Dad and Carol took Jeff and me to a Japanese restaurant that had tatami rooms, where you take off your shoes and sit on mats on the floor.

Then we went home and opened presents under the tree. We had agreed to celebrate that night, since we would be traveling the next morning — Jeff and me off to Connecticut, Dad and Carol off on their honeymoon in Mexico.

Carol had the biggest present. "Ooh, can I open this one first?" she asked.

"Sure," we said.

" 'To Carol, From Santa,' " Carol read on the tag. "Hmmmm."

With an excited smile, she ripped off the wrapping, opened a cardboard box, and reached inside.

"AAAAAAAAAUGH!" she screamed.

I thought Dad had bought her a live warthog or something.

She pulled out a huge lava lamp.

"*Gross,*" Jeff moaned.

"What do you think, dear?" Dad asked.

"It's . . . it's . . ." Carol shook her head in disbelief. "Horrible!"

She and Dad bellowed with laughter.

Jeff looked as if the sewer had just backed up under his nose.

But he didn't sneer for too long. Dad hopped up from the couch, disappeared into the garage, and carried in a brand-new bicycle, carefully wrapped in Christmas paper.

I have never heard that boy scream so loudly.

The only problem was, he kept trying to convince Dad to let him take it on the plane to Connecticut.

Me? I got two big presents. One was a pair of the coolest dangly earrings, made of bird of paradise feathers and lapis and all kinds of neat stuff. I was sure Carol had picked them out.

The other was an envelope. I opened it and took out a plain piece of folded paper — and another envelope, addressed to Dad at our house.

I unfolded the paper and read it:

John P. Schafer & Carol Olson

We O.U., Dawn Schafer, one (1) round-trip airplane ticket from Connecticut to Southern California, completely paid for, during your upcoming spring vacation, or at any other time that may be suitably convenient for you for said flight, which ticket will be purchased immediately upon your return of this voucher in the enclosed stamped, self-addressed envelope, providing the bottom stub is completed:

I, Dawn Schafer, being of sound mind and body, wish to fly on _____ and return on _____.   (date)
   (date)

Dawn

"Ohhhhhhh!" I gave Dad and Carol the biggest hugs.

I kept the letter on my bed table that night. I put it in my jacket pocket before we left for the airport. And as I wrote in my journal on the flight across the U.S., the letter was tucked safely into the pages.

I vowed it would be in Dad's mailbox when he and Carol returned from their honeymoon.

CHAPTER 22

SUZI

STONYBRUK DESMBER 25
HE DID IT !!!!
HE CAM !!!!
I NOO MY TRIK WUD WERK !!!!!

When I woke up Christmas morning, I didn't know where I was. It was still dark. All of the shapes in my room were wrong.

I got scared. I thought somebody had stolen me and put me in a strange place.

Then I knew what had happened. I was in my new house.

I got out of bed. Lindsey was snoring in the top bunk. I tiptoed out the door.

The light in the hallway was not on. The lights downstairs were not on. The whole house was creepy.

But I did not care. IT WAS CHRISTMAS!

I ran to the living room. Guess what?

The Christmas tree had lots of presents under it! And the cookies and milk were gone.

I crawled under the tree and looked at some of the presents. I can read a little. I read the name BUDDY on one present, and then SUZI on another.

"Yippee!" I screamed.

I was so happy. I danced the baloney dance. Here's how you do it: You run in place, shake your hands and head really fast at the same time, and say, "Baloney baloney baloney baloney baloney!" I've been doing that since I was little. It's funny. Buddy hates it.

"Suzi?"

Mommy was at the top of the stairs.

"It's Christmas!" I shouted.

"Ho ho ho! Merry Christmas!" a loud voice boomed.

At first I thought it was Santa — like, maybe he slept over. But it was Franklin. He walked up next to Mommy in his pajamas.

Franklin wears red pajamas every single night.

"Look! Look!" I cried out. "Santa came!"

Mommy smiled. "I guess your plan really worked, sweetheart."

"Yeaaaaaaaa!"

That was Lindsey. She slid down the bannister.

Madeleine ran downstairs next. Then Buddy and Taylor came up from the basement.

"Daddy! Pick me up!" Ryan cried from inside his room.

"Eee! Eee! Eee! Eee! Eee!" Marnie squealed.

"Buddy, you and Lindsey are in charge of passing out presents," Franklin said. Then he and Mommy went to take Marnie and Ryan out of their cribs.

I was trying to get my presents. But Taylor was pushing me. And Madeleine thought every single present was hers.

The room was way too crowded. I don't know if I like having so many brothers and sisters.

"Hey, you heard what Daddy said!" Lindsey yelled. "Everybody sit down. Back! Back!"

"Yeah," Buddy said. He pulled me away from the tree. By my collar. It hurt so much!

"Stop!" I said.

But Mommy and Franklin were walking downstairs with Marnie and Ryan. So we all behaved.

I was not mad at Buddy too much. But still, he should not have done that. I was the one who helped Santa find our house.

Know how I did it?

Well, I got the idea the day Logan was at our house. I told him Santa was not going to find us on Christmas. Logan tried to help me think. Then, all by myself, I thought up the perfect idea.

In school that day, my teacher read us Hansel and Gretel. I love that story. It's scary and happy. But Hansel and Gretel were so dumb. I mean, they shouldn't have left *bread crumbs* for their trail. Everyone knows birds eat them.

Then my teacher read us the story about the Minotaur. He was half-man and half-bull, and he lived inside a maze. Prince Theseus unrolled a ball of string through the maze, and after he killed the Minotaur, he just followed the string to get out. Now *that* was smart.

I thought about stretching a string from our old house to the new one. No way. Too long.

Then I thought, what does Santa like best of all?

Chocolate-chip cookies, of course.

Here's what I did. On Christmas Eve, Mommy and Franklin took us to dinner at the Washington Mall. Afterward they let us go to the ice-cream shop.

But I did not get ice cream. I got a small bag of chocolate-chip cookies.

I whispered my plan to Mommy. I told her not to tell Buddy. He would make fun of me.

We went home. Then Mommy told everyone that she was taking me on a drive, to do an errand.

We drove to our old house. I ate two of the cookies. I scrunched the rest up in the bag. Then I told Mommy to drive back to our new house really slowly.

On the way, I dropped the cookie crumbs out the window, a few at a time.

Guess what? I even had a little handful left over when we got home. I dumped them out under the living room window.

Buddy was in the living room. He saw me.

SUZI

When I went into the house, he was laughing. "You want the raccoons to spend Christmas with us?" he asked.

You know what? I didn't listen to him. Not one bit.

And now you know how Santa found my house. Just don't tell Buddy. He'll laugh at you, too.

CHAPTER 23

Dawn

Stoneybrook, December 25
Merry Christmas!
Here I am, back home.
The plane did not crash.
Connecticut is cold, wet,
and cloudy.
But I'm not complaining.
I'm with my mom, my
stepdad, my stepsister,
and my brother. I have
some fantastic memories.
I feel warm and happy.
Besides, how many
people get to have a
bicoastal holiday?

Dawn

Jeff woke up over Ohio (approximately) with a sore neck. Boy, was he cranky. A 10 on the Grumpometer.

He complained about the bumpy landing. He complained about the overhead compartment. He complained about the crowded aisles.

As we walked down the ramp toward the terminal, he mumbled to me, "Whatever you do, *don't cry*."

Me? I was ecstatic. I could see Mary Anne at the other end of the tunnel. She was waving so hard her hair was swishing back and forth.

"Don't cry . . . don't cry . . . don't cry . . ."

I ignored Jeff. I mean, puh-*leeze*. I was returning home after a long time away. My dad had gotten married, I had just been a bridesmaid, I was seeing my mom for the first time in months. What was I supposed to do? Shake hands and say, "How do you do?"

Before I could even think, my face was buried in the left shoulder of Mom's down parka. Jeff had the right side. We all swayed side-to-side. Mom was weeping with happiness. I was blubbering.

Jeff didn't shed a tear. But he also didn't get mad at me for crying. He didn't even seem to

have a stiff neck anymore. He was *beaming*.

Next Mary Anne and I had our hug-and-cry fest. Yes, we had just seen each other a few days before, but what does that matter?

I was home. It was a very big deal. Even Richard (Mary Anne's dad) gave me a big bear hug, and he's not exactly the cuddly type.

We practically flew home. The airport was empty, and so were the streets. Everyone was inside, enjoying the holiday.

In the car, Jeff started blabbing about the wedding. I wasn't going to bring it up. I figured Mom wouldn't feel too comfortable talking about it.

But she nodded and smiled. She laughed at the description of Dad's driving. (Maybe it's my imagination, but Richard seemed to drive much more carefully after hearing that.)

When we finally arrived in Stoneybrook and pulled onto Burnt Hill Road, my heart was racing.

"Oh, wow . . ." I had to gasp when I saw our house.

A huge sheet had been draped over the front door and decorated with holly and pine boughs. The words WELCOME, DAWN AND JEFF! were painted across it in red, green, and gold letters.

"Cool," Jeff said.

Richard parked, then opened the trunk. We lugged our suitcases to the front door.

The scent of pine hit me as we walked into the living room. In the corner opposite the fireplace was an enormous Christmas tree, glittering with ornaments and surrounded by presents.

"Who-o-o-oa!" Jeff dropped his suitcase and dove for the presents.

"Jeffrey, would you please pick this up?" Mom asked.

But Jeff was already sifting through the boxes, reading tags. Richard chuckled. "It's all right. First things first on Christmas Day, huh? I'll take his luggage in."

I had brought a duffel bag full of presents I'd bought for my family. I took it to the tree and emptied out the boxes.

Christmas II had begun. Jeff got a Swiss Army knife from Mom and Richard, which excited him even more than the bike had. I got a whole new collection of winter clothes — a ski sweater, lined pants, and a cashmere scarf.

"They're beautiful!" I exclaimed.

Richard smiled and looked at Mom. "We had an ulterior motive," he said.

"We figured they'll make you want to stay

in Connecticut," Mom added softly. She looked as if she were about to cry again.

Mary Anne was sniffling, too.

"Gag me," Jeff said.

After the present opening, my stomach decided to sing a Christmas carol: "The Little Drummer Boy." After a few refrains of *pa-rum-pum-pum-pum*, I realized I was starving.

The smells from the kitchen weren't helping, either.

By the time Richard said, "Shall we set the table?" I was trying hard not to drool.

Mary Anne and I ran to get the silverware. When we returned to the dining room, Richard and Jeff were putting a leaf in the table.

"What's that for?" I asked.

"Company," Richard replied.

"Oh," I said. "Great."

Company? On a special day like this? I was assuming it would be a nice, cozy, family Christmas.

I didn't complain. Mom and Richard had picked us up at the airport, bought all those nice presents, and gone through the trouble of preparing a feast. How could I be a bad sport?

Ding-dong. The doorbell rang as I was setting out the water glasses.

"Dawn, would you get it?" Mom called from the kitchen.

"Sure!"

As I pulled the door open, I heard a familiar voice say, "One, two, ready, go!"

Then many more voices sang out:

"Deck the halls with boughs of holly,
Fa-la-la-la-la, la-la-la-la,
Dawn is home, so we are jolly,
Fa-la-la-la-la, la-la-la-la!"

At that last line, Kristy, Claudia, Stacey, Jessi, and Mallory cracked up.

I stood there, my jaw hanging open. Mom, Richard, Jeff, and Mary Anne had gathered around me. "Is *this* the company?" I blurted out.

"Would I invite anyone else?" Mom said.

"Where's the food?" tactful Kristy asked.

"Save some for me!" Dad cried.

We ran into the dining room, chatting, squealing, laughing. And even though we didn't stop talking for hours, we managed to polish off every morsel of food.

I couldn't have imagined a better Christmas.

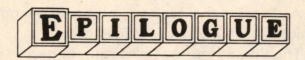

EPILOGUE

Today I got a post crad from Mr. Schafer and Carol. It was a pictur of a resturant with stroling gitarist. It said MEXICO LINDO. I gess that's the guys name. Sounds like a girl to me. Anyway, they said thanks and we woldn't' have been able to do it without you and all that. They also said that they forgot to thro out there flowers befor they left the house for the hunymoon.

That place is going to smell horible wen they get back. Rotting nashturshums and dead Stefan Otis, yuck!

I hop they don't tell Lile the Flowerist what they did. He has no sens of humor.

What a great Christmas.
Dawn and I did not
stop talking until 1:53 A.M.
When we finished catching
up on the week, we just
backtracked to the wedding,
and went over it
memory by memory.

Jeff came into my
room at one point. I
thought he was
going to complain, but
he sat on the floor and
listened. I think he
was lonely.

Unfortunately he fell
asleep, so we had to
carry him back to his
bedroom.

Just before we dozed
off, we imagined what
other weddings we'd be
going to someday.

I wondered if
Stacey's mom would
ever get married again.

Dawn hoped it would happen during the summer. Then she would recommend that mrs. McGill have a beach wedding.

You know what? I agreed.

I loved being a bridesmaid. I will never ever forget it.

But just in case I do, it looks like I'll be getting lots of reminders.

You see, my bridesmaids' gown came with something called a Dress Registry Form. You were supposed to fill out your name, address, phone number, dress size, etc. I figured it was like a warranty or something. So I sent it in right away.

Ever since then I have been getting all kinds of stuff in the mail. Monday it was an invitation to subscribe to a bridal magazine. Tuesday, two more bridal magazines and a catalog of discount household appliances. Wednesday someone from Good Housekeeping called me. Thursday it was Working Mom.

I think Friday was when I got the ad from the baby-stroller company.

Nothing arrived on Christmas. Thank goodness.

I guess I learned my lesson. No more forms.

Anyone want to join a baby-food-by-mail club?

I wish you all could have seen me as Santa. I was great. Really, I'm not being conceited. A lot of kids came back to see me two days in a row.

Ms. Javorsky says the job is open for me next year if I want it. But guess what? I heard through the grapevine that other stores were caught short. Maybe there will be more job opportunities next year.

I could set up a training program. A Santa camp. Seriously, being a good Santa takes technique.

Great idea, huh? What do you think, Kristy? Could you help?

GUESS WHO IS A CHILD PRODIGY IN MUSIC? WOULD YOU BELIEVE MY FIVE-YEAR-OLD BROTHER, HUNTER? HIS KINDERGARTEN TEACHER TOLD MY PARENTS HE HAS "A GREAT EAR AND PERFECT HANDS." (HUH?)

I DIDN'T THINK THAT MEANT MUCH, BUT MY MOM AND DAD ARE CONVINCED HE NEEDS TO START TAKING PIANO LESSONS.

CAN YOU FIGURE OUT WHAT COMES NEXT?

YOU GOT IT. AS OF WEDNESDAY, THE BARRETT/DEWITT LIVING ROOM WILL BE SHORT ONE PIANO.

AND I, LUGGIN' LOGAN, WILL BE BREAKING MY BACK OVER THAT TWO-TON MONSTER IN MY OWN LIVING ROOM.

A one hundred percent full Baby-sitters Club! Hurrah!
What a relief.
I think we did very, very well while Dawn was gone, when you think about it. But imagine what we'll be like now:
UNSTOPPABLE!
Okay, I know it's still the holiday vacation and all. And I love reminiscing about the weddings. But I think we should take advantage of our new strengths. Think of this as an opportunity to improve. Set new goals.
Remember that BSC promotional video we talked about making? I think it's a perfect topic for the next meeting. Think about it, guys.
Over and out.

Well, Ben and I exchanged Christmas presents. I gave him a beautiful winter hat.
He gave me a tape called "Ten Steps to Better Singing."
I think we need to have a talk.

I was sorry I missed everyone on Christmas Day. We went to my grandparents' house, which was fun.

I guess it was just as well. I'm going to have to get used to being the associate member again, huh?

Funny, back when Dawn left, I didn't think I could possibly have the time to go to all the meetings.

Now I wonder how I can go without them.

Oh, well, you may have to clear away some of the junk in your room, Claudia. You're not going to get rid of me that easily.

THIS IS WUT I ROT TO SANTA.
DEER SANTA.
THANK YOO FOR FINDWG MY
HOWS NOW YOO NO WARE I LIV.
DONT FOR GET NEX YEER BECAZ
I WONT LEEVE CRUMS ENY MOR
THAT IS LITERING
LUV SUZI

They did it again. Mary Anne and Dawn made so much noise Christmas night. I went in there room, but even that didn't shut them up.

They were so boring I fell asleep.

When I woke up they were carrying me to my room! They could bearly even lift me.

Anyway, Stonybrook isn't as bad as it used to be. I hung out with the Pike triplets the day after Christmas. They're fun.

Someday maybe I'll do what Dawn did. Like, come to Stonybrook for a semester. I just hope Dawn and Mary Anne learn to pipe down.

Maybe I could sleep in the barn.

That would be cool.

I am so glad everyone voted on my title for the wedding journals.

"Tale of Two Coasts."

It's catchy and mysterious. Although I thought Mary Anne's suggestion was great: "Christmas Wedding, Sea to Shining Sea." And I also liked Shannon's: "Holiday Vows."

At first I thought we'd just collate the pages. Then Dad mailed me all Claudia's photos, and they were so sensational. Especially the one where we're all smiling and Jeff is picking his nose. (You have to admit, it's funny!)

So we began including them. Then Kristy came up with some funny captions. And Claudia designed the most gorgeous covers, with a beach motif for the California album and a drawing of the church for the Stoneybrook one.

What a project. But they look wonderful. I know we'll read them again and again.

After all, I do plan to stay in Stoneybrook. At least until I use the plane tickets Dad promised me.

I think we have two weeks off in February....

About the Author

ANN M. MARTIN did *a lot* of baby-sitting when she was growing up in Princeton, New Jersey. She is a former editor of books for children, and was graduated from Smith College.

Ms. Martin lives in New York City with her cats, Mouse and Rosie. She likes ice cream and *I Love Lucy*; and she hates to cook.

Ann Martin's Apple Paperbacks include *Yours Turly, Shirley*; *Ten Kids, No Pets*; *With You and Without You*; *Bummer Summer*; and all the other books in the Baby-sitters Club series.

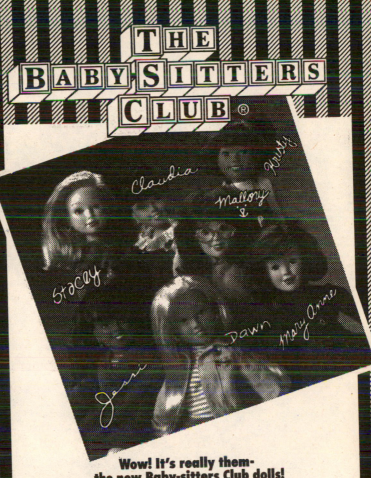

Stacey

Claudia

Mallory &

Kristy

Jessi

Dawn

Mary Anne

Wow! It's really them—
the new Baby-sitters Club dolls!

Your favorite Baby-sitters Club characters have come to life in these beautiful collector dolls. Each doll wears her own unique clothes and jewelry. They look just like the girls you have imagined! The dolls also come with their own individual stories in special edition booklets that you'll find nowhere else.

Look for the new Baby-sitters Club collection...
coming soon to a store near you!

Kenner.

The Baby-sitters Club © 1994 Scholastic, Inc. All Rights Reserved.   ® * Kenner, a Division of Tonka Corporation Cincinnati, Ohio 45202

The purchase of this item will result in a donation to the Ann M. Martin Foundation, dedicated to benefiting children, education and literacy programs, and the homeless.

Ann Martin wants *YOU*
to help name the new baby-sitter...and her twin.

Dear Diary,
I'm 13 now... finally in the 8th grade. My twin sister and I just moved here and this great group of girls asked me to join their baby-sitting club...

Name the twins and win a

THE BABY-SITTERS CLUB

book dedication!

Simply dream up the first and last names of the new baby-sitter and her twin sister (who's not in the BSC), and fill in the names on the coupon below. One lucky entry will be selected by Ann M. Martin and Scholastic Inc. The winning names will continue to be featured in the series starting next fall 1995, and the winner will have a future BSC book dedicated to her/him!

THE BSC NAME THE TWINS CONTEST

Name the new twins! (First and last, please)

_____ and _____

Name _____ Birthdate _____
                                                    M / D / Y

Street _____ City _____ State/Zip _____

BSCC1194

THE BABY-SITTERS CLUB®

by Ann M. Martin

More titles... ➤

The Baby-sitters Club titles continued...

☐ MG45659-8	#58 Stacey's Choice	$3.50
☐ MG45660-1	#59 Mallory Hates Boys (and Gym)	$3.50
☐ MG45662-8	#60 Mary Anne's Makeover	$3.50
☐ MG45663-6	#61 Jessi's and the Awful Secret	$3.50
☐ MG45664-4	#62 Kristy and the Worst Kid Ever	$3.50
☐ MG45665-2	#63 Claudia's Freind Friend	$3.50
☐ MG45666-0	#64 Dawn's Family Feud	$3.50
☐ MG45667-9	#65 Stacey's Big Crush	$3.50
☐ MG47004-3	#66 Maid Mary Anne	$3.50
☐ MG47005-1	#67 Dawn's Big Move	$3.50
☐ MG47006-X	#68 Jessi and the Bad Baby-Sitter	$3.50
☐ MG47007-8	#69 Get Well Soon, Mallory!	$3.50
☐ MG47008-6	#70 Stacey and the Cheerleaders	$3.50
☐ MG47009-4	#71 Claudia and the Perfect Boy	$3.50
☐ MG47010-8	#72 Dawn and the We Love Kids Club	$3.50
☐ MG45575-3	Logan's Story Special Edition Readers' Request	$3.25
☐ MG47118-X	Logan Bruno, Boy Baby-sitter Special Edition Readers' Request	$3.50
☐ MG44240-6	Baby-sitters on Board! Super Special #1	$3.95
☐ MG44239-2	Baby-sitters' Summer Vacation Super Special #2	$3.95
☐ MG43973-1	Baby-sitters' Winter Vacation Super Special #3	$3.95
☐ MG42493-9	Baby-sitters' Island Adventure Super Special #4	$3.95
☐ MG43575-2	California Girls! Super Special #5	$3.95
☐ MG43576-0	New York, New York! Super Special #6	$3.95
☐ MG44963-X	Snowbound Super Special #7	$3.95
☐ MG44962-X	Baby-sitters at Shadow Lake Super Special #8	$3.95
☐ MG45661-X	Starring the Baby-sitters Club Super Special #9	$3.95
☐ MG45674-1	Sea City, Here We Come! Super Special #10	$3.95

Available wherever you buy books...or use this order form.

Scholastic Inc., P.O. Box 7502, 2931 E. McCarty Street, Jefferson City, MO 65102

Please send me the books I have checked above. I am enclosing $_____
(please add $2.00 to cover shipping and handling). Send check or money order - no
cash or C.O.D.s please.

Name _____ Birthdate_____

Address _____

City_____ State/Zip _____

Please allow four to six weeks for delivery. Offer good in the U.S. only. Sorry, mail orders are not
available to residents of Canada. Prices subject to change.

BSC993